BLACK GOLD IN NORTH DAKOTA

COOPER SMITH BOOK 2

JOE FIELD

D1528114

Published by PAUL BUNYAN PUBLISHING, Minnesota

CONTENTS

*This is for my beLoVeD family
and the kindred spirits of the North Star State*

CHAPTER 1

Williston, North Dakota

Gabby Hanson wiped the sweat off of her forehead with a towel as her legs raced to keep pace with the treadmill's spinning belt. The treadmill's red display lights showed her speed at seven miles per hour with a three percent incline. She was fifty minutes into her workout with ten hard minutes to go. She concentrated on Taylor Swift's voice in her headphones, singing about the year 1989. Gabby preferred to run outside, but it was a December night in northwest North Dakota.

Good luck with that, thought Gabby.

The only movement around here at night came from oil drills, roughnecks, and strippers. Gabby didn't associate with any of those hell-raisers, so she found herself running alone on a Saturday night at the barren Williston Area Recreation Center.

The locals called the community's new state-of-the-art fitness center the "ARC," partly to shorten the long name but mostly as a pun on the gigantic interior wood wall that ran nearly the full length of the 650-foot center hallway, which was on scale with Noah's ark. At seventy-six million dollars, the facility was the largest and most expensive city-owned indoor recreation center in the country. As one of Williston's city council members, Gabby had helped promote a yes-vote back in 2011 for a one-percent sales tax increase to help pay for the ARC. She was proud when the measure passed, but over time she grew disgusted by all the roughnecks who converged on the ARC to wash their oil filth off after a day on the drill.

These treadmills and weights are pretty much just a cover for the world's most expensive shower house.

Gabby had seen it one too many times. The roughnecks would come into the ARC covered in black oil grease from head to toe, and leave thirty minutes later looking clean and refreshed.

Then it was straight to the bars or strip clubs downtown. The few that were loyal to their wives would head back to their man camps to rest up before hitting the drills hard again in the morning.

Just as she was about to slow to a jog, Gabby looked up and saw two roughnecks walk in. *Great, here we go again.* Gabby kept her pace up so the men wouldn't know she was finishing her workout.

She recognized one of them. He reminded her of the Marlboro Man. Tall and strapping, he wore a tan cowboy hat and a thick work jacket over a red and black flannel shirt. His cowboy boots left tracks on the ARC's clean floor. The second man was shorter, and stocky. Built like a bulldog. He was either wearing all black, or his entire outfit was stained through with grease. Bulldog looked more like the hillbilly variety, maybe from Louisiana or Mississippi.

As the men neared, Gabby could see patches of exposed white skin on their faces and hands, which were mostly hidden beneath a black oil slick. She tried to place where she had seen Marlboro. He was staring right at her. Despite the sweat dripping from her brow, a shiver ran through her body at the way he looked at her.

Like she was an object. *His object.*

Instead of her planned cool-down jog, Gabby picked up her pace and looked away from the roughnecks. Her legs had become jelly minutes before, but there was no way she was stopping now. When she turned her head back, Bulldog was standing next to her treadmill, with Marlboro a few feet behind him.

Bulldog waved at Gabby and motioned for her to take her headphones off.

Just go take your shower and leave me alone. She pointed down to the treadmill to show she was busy.

Bulldog again motioned for her to take off her headphones.

You've got to be kidding me. Gabby grabbed the treadmill rails with her hands and lifted her legs off to either side of the belt as it continued to spin. She reluctantly took off her headphones. "Can I help you?"

"Well, pretty lady, that depends on what you're doing later tonight." Bulldog's accent was clearly Southern, with a twang like an out-of-tune banjo. He snickered as he looked back at Marlboro; Gabby followed his glance and caught the taller man gazing right into her eyes over Bulldog's shoulder.

"Leave me alone—I'm trying to work out here." Gabby moved her headphones back up toward her ears.

Bulldog lifted his hands quickly in defense. "Wait just a minute. I do apologize for being so up front. And, I realize I look like a swamp creature right now, but once I get cleaned up I'll come back and we can make proper introductions. How does that sound?"

Gabby ignored his comments and put her headphones back in her ears before she began running again. She could see Bulldog mouth, "feisty."

Get bent, loser.

Bulldog gestured toward the shower rooms and then back to Gabby's treadmill, suggesting he was coming back to talk to her after his shower. With that, the roughnecks turned to walk toward the locker room. Marlboro gazed at Gabby one more time before he followed Bulldog to the showers.

Gabby's skin crawled.

How did my sweet hometown come to this?

Gabby longed for the Williston of her youth. Back then, the town had a simple routine and rhythm that provided stability and comfort. It was a quiet town where you knew everyone's name and business. Williston natives looked forward to the Friday fish fry at Saint Joseph's church, and talked about Williston High's prospects on the gridiron that fall. When the oil money and men came in, people touted it as progress and positive change. To Gabby, the change came too fast and she felt hoodwinked by outsiders who seemed to care only about making fast money. She hated the fact that these roughnecks had invaded her backyard to pillage the land and corrupt the town. Most of all, she hated that these horny toads constantly tried to pick her up. Sure, she was a single woman in her mid-twenties, with what most of her friends would describe as good looks. Gabby had fair skin, with shoulder-length strawberry-blonde hair. She noticed people were drawn to her bright sea-green eyes, and the dimples and freckles on her cheeks radiated youthful energy when she smiled. Her long hours in the gym helped her body stay slender and toned.

But where do these roughnecks get off trying to hit on me while I am exercising? I work on the city council for Pete's sake, not on some pole down on Main Street.

Once they were out of sight, Gabby made a beeline for the women's locker room. She skipped the shower and quickly changed into her street clothes, grabbing her gym bag from the locker on her way out. She raced out of the locker room to the front of the ARC; thankfully, she didn't see either of the men. As she exited, the vicious Dakota wind struck her in the face. She pulled a scarf out of her bag. Pressing it against her nose and cheeks, she strode toward her white Volkswagen Jetta, which stood out under one of the ARC parking lot's lights. It was the only car among a few scattered pickup trucks and one RV camper.

Gabby reached her car door quickly, but her cold hands fumbled with the unlock button on her key fob and the trunk popped open instead. Gabby cursed to herself as she walked around the back of her vehicle. Just as she reached up to close the trunk she heard loud footsteps behind her. She turned around in time to see two large figures running toward her, one from either side of the RV. They were the two roughnecks from inside, and they were still covered in oil.

Marlboro reached for her first, but she dodged his grasp. Gabby turned to run toward the ARC, but Bulldog blocked her path. She cried out for help, but there was no one around. She juked quickly to her left. Marlboro was too fast; he stretched his right arm and caught hold of Gabby's left wrist. His grip was strong but his hand was greasy, and Gabby started to slide her wrist out. She used the momentum to swing the bag in her right hand toward his head. He effortlessly grabbed the bag with his free hand and pulled her in close to him.

Then he squeezed her. A crushing bear hug.

Gabby instinctively kneed him hard in the groin, and he released his hold and fell back.

Bulldog was now upon her and was choking her from behind with her own scarf. Gabby tried kicking back at him, but he was too close. She impulsively reached her hands up to the scarf to pull it down so she could get the air she needed. As she did, Bulldog pulled the scarf down harder with his left hand and snaked his right arm around her waist. She tried to elbow him but had no leverage.

Marlboro recovered and rushed up to Gabby. He wrapped his bulky right arm around her neck and put her in a tight headlock as he took her from Bulldog. Marlboro kept the headlock tense as he dragged her toward the RV. Gabby thrashed her legs, but it was useless; he was too strong. Bulldog ran around them and opened the RV's side door. Marlboro lifted her into the RV, and as the door slammed shut Gabby's world went black.

CHAPTER 2

Dickinson, North Dakota

❝ I suppose you want the first go at her," said Doyle. He was sitting in the RV's front passenger seat and was looking back at the floor where the woman was still passed out. Doyle had been waiting for over two hours for Nash to pull the RV over so he could fool around with her.

"No," replied Nash.

"So… that means I get to go first?" Doyle shifted excitedly in his seat.

"No, the woman is not to be touched," said Nash. There was no hint of negotiation in his tone.

"What do you mean?" Doyle whined.

"I mean exactly what I said. The woman is not to be touched." Nash turned the RV down a gravel road. "Listen, this woman has done more to hurt us oil guys than anyone else in all of North Dakota."

"What has she done?"

"Don't you follow any of the local news?" Nash shook his head. *Nothing but a backwater Louisiana redneck,* he thought. "She is on the Williston City Council, and is adamantly opposed to the oil industry. Her goal is to make life harder than it already is for newcomers like us. She wants to destroy our livelihood and send us all back to the dirty south."

"Really?" Doyle's excitement was beginning to turn over to anger.

"Yes, really. Do you want to go back down to Louisiana and spend your days doing God knows what to make a buck? Or do you want to stay and continue to print money here in North Dakota?" Nash turned the RV's lights to low beam as they came into a clearing. An old abandoned oil drill stood off in the distance.

"Is that why we took her? To take care of her?"

"Yes."

Doyle was now at the edge of his seat. "Can't we just have some fun with her first before we kill her? It would be such a waste."

"The final answer is no. Now grab your gloves; we're almost there."

"Almost where?" asked Doyle.

Nash slowed the RV to a crawl and pulled up next to the old drill. "Right here. We are going to go dig a hole behind this drill and bury her."

"*Alive?*"

"Yes."

Doyle's eyes grew wide. "I don't know…. It's kind of cold out there." He rubbed the back of his neck. "How are we going to dig a hole?"

Nash reached behind Doyle's seat and grabbed two blowtorches. He handed one to Doyle, who scrunched his forehead as he inspected it.

"It's a blowtorch," said Nash. "We'll use it to thaw the ground. After it softens, I'll take the pickaxe and do the heavy hitting to break up the soil. You'll follow behind with the shovel. She's pretty small, so we won't have to dig for long. Plus, there is a snowstorm coming in the next few days that will cover the hole until spring. That's all the time we need."

Doyle took one more look back at Gabby, then he looked over at Nash, and finally out the RV's front window at the drill. "Well, shoot. Let's get this over with."

With that, the two men stepped out of the RV to dig Gabby's grave.

***

Gabby attempted to sit up, but her head felt like a ton of bricks. As she tried to clear the fog from her mind, she felt the cold floor beneath her and heard an engine running. She slowly opened one eye and saw she was on the floor of an RV. After a few moments, she started to remember the confrontation in the parking lot. She craned her neck up, but fell back over as her head started to spin again.

The roughnecks. What did those devils do to me?

Gabby's mind started to fill up with horrible thoughts. She looked down and saw she was still fully clothed, wearing the street clothes she put on after her workout.

They haven't abused my body yet, but when? Where are they?

Gabby slowly shifted her head from side-to-side as she looked around. She was in a standard RV equipped with a table, a small kitchen, and a bed above the driver's seat. Both of the front seats were empty, but she could see two figures silhouetted by the RV's lights moving around outside. The taller one was swinging something toward the ground. *Was it an axe?* The other was scooping dirt up with a shovel.

Are they digging something up? Then Gabby's gut wrenched as she realized, *I'm dead. They are going to rape me, kill me, and then bury my body. Never to be found again.*

***

The wind picked up and pierced the men's faces and hands. "Can we stop already?" Doyle threw out another load of dirt from the hole he was now standing in, already up to his waist. "This is crazy, and I'm freezing."

"You'll be done when I say so," replied Nash evenly.

This is the last time I hire a Cajun to do my dirty work, thought Nash.

"Who made you the boss?" asked Doyle.

"Remember who is paying you for your help tonight," said Nash. "And as long as I'm paying for your services, you'll shut up, do as you're told, and finish digging this hole."

Doyle rolled his eyes and set his shovel down. "I'm going to go take a leak quick in the RV and I'll be right back."

"Come on, man." Nash shook his head at Doyle. "Okay, just do that last corner really quick. When you finish you can go drain your bladder." Nash pointed to the far back corner of the hole.

"Okay, boss. Whatever you say." Doyle turned his back on Nash and started scooping out the rear corner of the hole.

As Doyle turned around, Nash lifted his pickaxe high above his head and swung down with all his force. It landed squarely on the base of Doyle's neck. Doyle's body collapsed into the hole. Unmoving, he let out his last remaining gasp for air as Nash rocked and ripped the pickaxe from his spine.

Nash threw the pickaxe down and yanked the shovel out from beneath Doyle's dead body. He rummaged through Doyle's pockets until he found the dead man's keys and wallet, which he kept. Nash then began to toss the loose dirt back into the hole on top of Doyle.

You dumb fool, Nash thought. *You just fell for the oldest trick in the West, and now the woman's all mine.*

***

Gabby looked on in terror as Marlboro swung the pickaxe down on Bulldog's back. Bulldog went limp and Marlboro started covering his body with dirt. *If he is willing to kill his own partner, what will he do to me?*

Gabby was now up on all fours, slowly regaining her motor skills. *They must have drugged me,* she thought as she fought the dizziness. She wanted to make a run for it, but she had no idea where she was. Plus, Marlboro would easily be able to catch her—and even if she escaped she would likely freeze to death. No, her only option was to drive away.

Crawling toward the driver's seat, Gabby kept her eyes glued to Marlboro as he continued to bury Bulldog. Her adrenaline spiked—it was now or never. The RV continued to idle as she slid into the seat. She looked at the controls and tried to concentrate. She had never driven an RV before, but she found what looked to be the gearshift. She put it into drive and hit the accelerator hard with her foot.

The RV's tires spun on the gravel for a second, and then it lunged forward. Marlboro snapped his head around just in time to dive out of the RV's way.

Gabby impulsively tried to turn the wheels to hit him. The front left tire slid sideways into Bulldog's grave, causing the RV to bounce violently up and over the dead man's body in the hole below.

Losing control of the RV, Gabby thrust her foot toward the brakes but hit the gas pedal. The RV accelerated toward the old oil drill platform. Gabby tried to reach up for the seatbelt, but was too late. The force of the impact flung Gabby's body forward, and her head smacked the front windshield. The glass splintered and her body slumped back down between the two front seats. She was out cold.

CHAPTER 3

Williston, North Dakota

The bumper sticker on the red pickup truck in front of Cooper Smith read *oil field trash and proud of it.* A black pickup truck behind him insisted on hugging his rear bumper despite the traffic jam. Cooper tried to ignore him by taking another long drag from his American Spirit cigarette.

My old friend, Mr. Nicotine. Good to have you back.

He blew the smoke out of a cracked window in his trusty blue Jeep Wrangler, christened *Wellstone* after the late Senator Paul Wellstone of Minnesota. It idled on Highway 2 near Williston, which might as well have been Interstate 90 in Chicago during rush hour. White clouds streamed out from the mufflers on the vehicles as the warm engine exhaust hit the cool December air. Wellstone had crept forward a mere mile in the last half hour. The local news reported that a semi tractor-trailer had jack-knifed across the road and was blocking traffic in both directions.

Not a good omen for the trip, Cooper thought.

Cooper finished his cigarette and lowered his window. The arctic-like wind hit him in the face, and he quickly flicked the cigarette onto the pavement and closed the window tight. He took a drink of coffee from his thermos and grabbed another piece of black licorice from the open bag in his lap.

My three favorite vices: cigarettes, licorice, and coffee. These three trusted friends could get me through any assignment.

As Cooper put his coffee back in the cup holder, he spilled a little bit of it on his pants. He looked down, shrugged it off, and then laughed when he thought about his attire. He knew it was cheesy, but he couldn't help making a stop at a Mills Fleet Farm store on his way out of town. He wore a black stocking hat, a blue and white flannel shirt, a winter jacket, and heavy-duty work jeans. All made by Carhartt.

Like a walking Carhartt mannequin. They should pay me to wear all this gear.

The only thing that wasn't Carhartt was his trusty Red Wing boots. Made in Red Wing, Minnesota, the reliable boots kept his feet warm and supported even in the coldest North Dakota weather. Cooper looked back up when the black pickup truck honked at him again from behind, urging Cooper to inch forward some more.

What does two inches get you, buddy? Cooper shot him a look in his rearview mirror.

This wasn't exactly the welcome-home assignment Cooper had been looking forward to following his month-long European honeymoon with his new bride, Soojin. They'd had the time of their lives as they strolled down the streets of Paris, danced with the locals in Munich, sipped on cappuccinos in Rome, drank excessive amounts of *vino* in Tuscany, and made love in seven different countries. Cooper had even rediscovered his love of black licorice in its homeland, Holland. Soojin didn't mind red licorice, but she couldn't understand how he could eat the black stuff. It was the most memorable trip of Cooper's life, and if not for all the weight he had gained, he could have stayed forever.

One sore spot on the honeymoon was Cooper's relapse into smoking—a habit he had given up a few years before he met Soojin.

It had started innocently enough with a few celebratory cigars at his wedding, then a few more in Italy. From there, the nicotine addiction began creeping back, and by the end of the trip, Cooper was going out late at night in search of a secret smoke.

Secret, because Soojin hated it.

It was turning out to be a sore spot in their young union, but Cooper was only smoking a few cigarettes a day since returning to Minnesota—usually just on breaks at work, and never around Soojin. Plus, he was smoking the natural American Spirits cigarettes, which supposedly didn't have all the extra additives.

And now my world revolves around western North Dakota. At least I can smoke out here to stay warm and pass the time.

Before heading out to North Dakota, Cooper had attended a preparation meeting back at Minnesota Public Radio headquarters in Saint Paul with his editor, Bill Anderson. *Wild Bill*, as the reporters called him, was in true form for that meeting as he questioned Cooper's commitment and loyalty to MPR following his month-long honeymoon. Cooper assured Bill he would not be getting married again anytime soon so there was no need to worry about other extended vacations. As usual, Cooper's sarcastic remarks won him a fiery retort from Wild Bill.

"You young punks are all the same." Bill's face burned bright red. "You think the world should be handed to you on a silver spoon. You need your little boutique coffee, and your hipster boots, and your hair gel. Why the hell do you need so much hair gel? Would you like a more flexible work schedule? Okay, I can accommodate. How does working from home *permanently* sound to you? Don't bother picking up your last check, either, I'll send it with your pink slip in the mail."

"Bill, to be fair—"

"You better grab your hair gel and get out to North Dakota quick, like tomorrow morning. I've waited long enough for this. We *need* to get the Bakken oil story. I've heard rumors that the oil boom is about to go bust and I want you to get a story worthy of this newsroom." Bill suddenly stood up from his desk and looked outside his window at the traffic out on the street. "All the majors are heading out there, including the *New York Times*. But, don't think for one moment I want some *NYT* policy wonk article. *You* need to go out there and tell the stories of the actual people on the ground. I'm talking about original stories of the people in western North Dakota affected by the oil boom. And, like I always say, the story needs to have—"

"Breadth and depth. I got it, Bill. No need to worry about a thing, I'll get you the story."

Cooper thought Bill would cut him some slack following his successful *Brown Sugar in Minnesota* series, which highlighted the heroin epidemic in Minnesota. That story ultimately helped authorities take down a major drug ring in the state. It wasn't enough for Wild Bill, and now Cooper knew one thing was true about editors.

They have shorter memories than squirrel monkeys.

Another loud honk from the black pickup truck brought Cooper back to the present. He looked closer in his rearview mirror and could see a man wearing a blue stocking hat behind the wheel of his truck making hand gestures for Cooper to move ahead. Cooper gave a vague wave of acknowledgement and eased slowly onto the gas, antagonizing the tailgater even more by not speeding up fast enough. Cooper could see the man rip his hat off and show Cooper how long his middle finger was when raised from a closed fist.

Classy. Real classy.

Cooper saw a Walmart sign up ahead on the right. A perfect escape so the black pickup could pass him. As he pulled into the parking lot, Cooper wondered what Lewis and

Clark would think of this town, which they visited back in 1804, now. They had spent a wretched winter here as they erected walls and met with Sacajawea to prepare for what they thought would be their demise. And, what would Cooper's beloved Teddy Roosevelt have said about this area of western North Dakota, a place that was once his refuge after the loss of his wife and mother? They would probably be as culture shocked as Cooper was as he looked up at the enormous Walmart logo that greeted his arrival.

Endless rows of parked pickup trucks and RV campers filled the lot. Cooper pulled Wellstone into an open space. He looked over toward his passenger side window, and to his disgust he saw the black pickup truck park next to him. The man put his hat back on, got out of his vehicle and spat chewing tobacco onto Wellstone's passenger window, leaving a dark streak. The man had a husky build and a thick black mustache. After a lingering glare, the mustached man turned and walked toward the front door of the Walmart.

Who pissed in that guy's cereal this morning?

Cooper was curious about what the inside of the Walmart might look like. He had heard stories about barren shelves and mind-numbingly long lines. But, with his tobacco-spitting friend inside, he decided to stay in his vehicle and have another smoke.

As he lit up, he watched the spit slide down his window. When it reached the bottom, Cooper turned and looked out his windshield, noticing an electronic billboard directly in front of him. It featured bright advertisements that rotated every ten to twenty seconds. The first one was from Walmart, and it offered prospective employees a $500 signing bonus and $18 per hour for stocking positions. *Shoot, that's more than I make at MPR.* The next advertisement was for new Ford pickup trucks. The third display caused Cooper's jaw to drop.

That's not possible.

It was a public service announcement from the Williams County Sherriff's department. They were offering a five thousand dollar reward for anyone who could provide details that would lead to the whereabouts of a missing person. Cooper had seen similar billboards countless times, but this was the first one that had ever mattered to him. The face and name on the billboard belonged to Gabby Hanson, one of Soojin's best friends and a bridesmaid at their recent wedding.

***

"**Soojin, I—I** have something to tell you," Cooper stammered into his phone.

"Coop, what is it?"

"It's bad news." Cooper paused. "I'm sitting here in a parking lot in Williston watching a rotating digital billboard . . . ."

"What is it?" Soojin's voice wavered.

"It's Gabby."

"What about her?"

"She's gone missing, it looks like she may have been kidnapped."

Soojin let out a gasp just before Cooper heard a clatter.

"Are you there? Hun, are you there?"

"Sorry, I dropped my phone." Soojin's breath was ragged. "Are you sure?"

"I've watched the same notice loop through five times now," Cooper said. "I don't have many details, but I'm going to head down to the sheriff's office to see what I can find out."

"We have to find her," said Soojin. "I can be there tonight. I'll catch the next plane out of the Twin Cities."

"Just wait a minute. Let me talk to the authorities before you head out here, and I'll call you right back. Then we can make a decision on the best course of action."

"Get over there quick," Soojin said. "I'll start looking online to see what the local news is saying."

Cooper had a terrible feeling in his gut as he hung up the phone. Soojin and Gabby had been roommates for four years at the University of Minnesota's main campus in the Twin Cities. They had bonded quickly when they learned they had both lost parents. Soojin had lost her mother to breast cancer when she was seven, and Gabby lost both her parents in a car accident when she was nine. Gabby had been raised by her grandfather, long-time North Dakota state senator, Mark Hanson. Senator Hanson ignited a political spark in Gabby that was further strengthened through her connection with Soojin. The two of them were strong voices on the U of M campus and in the Twin Cities community. They joked that they would both be the first female governors of their respective states, which wasn't so farfetched.

Until Gabby went missing.

Cooper drove Wellstone across the parking lot toward the billboard so he could read the text on the bottom. He looked up at Gabby's picture as it flashed and then quickly took down the number and address of the sheriff's office. Cooper checked his map for the location and put Wellstone back into drive.

As the Jeep sprang forward, he noticed out of his peripheral vision that a vehicle was accelerating right toward his rear passenger-side window. It was too late to react, as the vehicle struck Wellstone and jolted the Jeep sideways. Cooper tried to turn the wheel, but he couldn't stop the momentum as Wellstone slammed into a parked RV. Cooper's seatbelt locked as his airbag popped out and struck his face.

When the airbag had settled, Cooper grabbed for the door handle to get out, but stopped. He heard a man shouting and running toward the Jeep. Cooper locked his door as the man reached for the handle. Cooper could see around the airbag that it was the Mustache Man with the blue hat from the black pickup truck. His face was beet red as he pounded on Cooper's window.

"Get out here right now, I'm going to kill you!" Mustache screamed.

Cooper tried to put his vehicle back into drive, but it was wedged too tightly between the RV and pickup truck. Mustache sprinted back around to his pickup truck and Cooper could see him grab something out of the truck bed—a crowbar. As Mustache came back to the driver's side window, Cooper slid around the airbag and over the center console to the rear passenger side so he could escape.

Mustache smashed the driver's side window with his crowbar. Glass shattered into the Jeep. Cooper grabbed the only weapon he kept in the vehicle, a small tomahawk under the rear seat. He pulled off the cover and jumped out the rear passenger side door.

Mustache sprinted back around his truck with the crowbar to meet Cooper on the other side. Just as Mustache rounded his truck, a police car's sirens whistled out as it shot across the parking lot straight toward them.

"Drop your weapons," boomed a voice over a speaker from the police car.

Cooper and Mustache both stopped and immediately dropped their weapons to the ground. Cooper raised his hands up over his head. The other man, now ten feet away from Cooper, also reluctantly lifted his hands.

"You better hope they put us in separate cells, or you're done for," said Mustache.

He spat once more at Cooper just as the police car stopped and two officers exited the vehicle with guns drawn.

Welcome to Williston, Cooper.

CHAPTER 4

Bismarck, North Dakota

The North Dakota governor's residence was just that—a residence. While most states had prominent gubernatorial mansions, the Peace Garden State settled for an unassuming, one-story brick house near the state's capitol building. First built in 1960, the home had suffered its fair share of wear and tear with a few stopgap renovations to keep it functional. A bipartisan group of North Dakotan congressmen had expressed interest in using new state revenues from oil taxation to build a new governor's residence, and they planned to put forward a bill in the upcoming 2015 session.

The primary beneficiary of this new bill, a man named Rick Simmons, was elected in 2010 as the thirty-second governor of North Dakota. Simmons crafted a public image of a tee-totaling, straight-and-narrow Ronald Reagan Republican while privately enjoying fine whiskey, cigars, and women not named Mrs. Simmons.

The wind howled outside the governor's residence as the temperature dropped and clouds moved in to block the full moon. Simmons sat back in a large leather chair with his feet up on his dark, wood-paneled executive desk. His Richard Nixon bobblehead doll sat on his desktop. The room was dark, except for the light illuminated from the fireplace. The room was lined with books on floor-to-ceiling bookshelves, which were purely decorative. Simmons avoided reading at all costs. He hated it so much he had his secretary read important bills to him out loud while he smoked cigars.

Simmons was in his forties, as short as he was wide, with salt-and-pepper hair. He hid his deep-set eyes behind hipster glasses—his ploy for relating to his younger constituents.

He took a long pull from his cigar and slowly exhaled, glancing across the desk at Nate Thompson, his lieutenant governor. "Have you seen Bob's new intern?"

"Not yet." Thompson had been elected with Simmons in the Republican Party's banner 2010 election year. "But I heard she's a total knockout. What is Bob putting in the water up there in Grand Forks to produce such beautiful women?"

While Simmons was short and chubby, Thompson was tall and bony. He attributed his physique to genetics and his obsession with running. He had won his age category in the Fargo Marathon each of the last six years. He was four years younger than Simmons, and the two politicians had secretly agreed to a two-term Simmons administration, followed by a Thompson succession.

"I guess when you are elected to the state senate for twenty years, the women come running," said Simmons.

"As if a whole bottle of Viagra could even help a guy like that," replied Thompson.

The men snickered as Thompson stood up and poured two more glasses of whiskey.

"What do you know about her?" asked Simmons.

"Not too much. I heard she graduated from UND in May with a political science major. Looking to make a career out of politics."

"Oh, really . . ." Simmons set down his glass as his eyebrows rose. "See what you can do about arranging an informal meet-and-greet between her and me. *Informal* being the key word." Simmons winked at Thompson.

"I'll see what I can do." Thompson took out his phone and wrote himself a reminder.

"Speaking of old geezers," said Simmons, "I was briefed today by the highway patrol about old Senator Hanson, and the situation with his granddaughter. What's the plan to mitigate risk here?"

"You mean, in regards to the money?"

"Of course."

Thompson took a big swig of his drink and set it down on the table next to him. "Well, Hanson took the money willingly and looked the other way when those oil companies fracked the hell out of protected lands. He is in too deep now."

"Yes, but I'm afraid this incident with his precious granddaughter and those idiot roughnecks might put him over the edge. You know, make him talk." Simmons set his cigar down and started to tap his fingers on his desk.

"Don't worry, he isn't going to bring the whole ship down over this. He would be committing career suicide, and worse, he would send us all to jail, himself included. We all made an agreement, and he will stick by it."

"You're from his hometown and you served with him in the capital for years," Simmons said. "Can you use your history with him to keep him quiet? I don't want this to get away from us. We've come too far, and there is so much more money to be made."

"I'll reach out to him tomorrow. Where do the police think Gabby is?"

"They haven't got a clue. It's a terrible thought, but she's probably already dead in a ditch somewhere, and I'm sure that roughneck is long gone."

"Do you want to call for extra police and rescue resources to help with the search?"

Simmons finished off his drink and turned his glass over so the rim was down on the table. Then he pushed Nixon's head down with his index finger and watched it bob.

Nixon gave him his mischievous smile with his signature peace signs extended from his body. "Nah, there's no use. That blizzard is going to hit sometime tonight or early in the morning. Tell them all to go home and to brace for the storm. I'm going to bed."

CHAPTER 5

The Louisiana Bayou

A houseboat sat perfectly still on top of green, swampy water, tucked tightly between patches of cypress trees, Spanish moss dangling down on its roof and sides. A sliver of light from a high noon sun hit one of the windows on the houseboat's ceiling, and for a few minutes it illuminated the inside. It would be the only natural light inside the houseboat all day.

Tucked away in a remote section of the Louisiana bayou south of the city of Houma, the boat was accessible only by water. At Nash's request, Doyle had described the location in painstaking detail after bragging about how he used to take women out there. Doyle even drew Nash a map to the location from a marina at the edge of Houma where his houseboat was docked.

Nearly thirty-six hours before, Nash had stolen a vehicle from the parking lot at the Dickinson Theodore Roosevelt Regional Airport. He placed an unconscious Gabby under some blankets in the backseat and headed south toward Houma. He had worried the entire drive about Doyle's houseboat, and whether it had been moved, or if the keys he swiped from Doyle's coat would actually work. He also worried about being pulled over by police, but with his former law enforcement training he knew how to avoid detection. He religiously maintained the speed limit, avoided toll roads and places with cameras, and took shot after shot of five-hour energy drinks to keep himself going while time was still on his side. He also hoped the car's owner was gone for the holidays and that no one would notice it missing from the airport parking lot until long after Nash was done with it.

To his relief, he arrived uneventfully in Houma late at night. The houseboat was located exactly where Doyle told him it would be. He hid the stolen vehicle under a tarp at a nearby vacant warehouse and carried a comatose Gabby to the houseboat by way of Doyle's crude map to the middle of nowhere.

Nash couldn't think of a more terrible place to live than the bayous of Louisiana. Except for the fact that Gabby—*his* Gabby—was now with him. He had to fight the irresistible urge to go lay next to her. She was the most beautiful woman he had ever laid eyes on, with her radiant face and heart melting, bright green eyes.

Her body was a perfect temple, a symbol of all that was right in this world.

Nash knew it from afar, but up close he could confirm that she had small freckles on her cheeks and a beauty mark above her lip.

She was heavenly.

To pass the time while he waited for Gabby to wake up from the tranquilizers, Nash began a list of words to describe the bayou. Writing lists was one of his obsessions. He always chose seven things per category. It couldn't be six or eight; it *had* to be exactly seven. He could write additional comments in parenthesis after the word, but only if it was a seven-word comment. It drove his parents and teachers crazy during his childhood.

THE BAYOU:
1. Fiery Gates of Hell
2. Sticky Air
3. Backwater
4. A Redneck's Paradise (rest in peace hillbilly Doyle, nice houseboat)

5. Wicked Souls
6. Alligators Haven
7. Mosquitos (those vile little angry blood-sucking vampires)

Those words describe my hell, Nash thought. *And it's the last place on earth that anyone would ever expect a Texas Ranger, turned North Dakota roughneck, to be at this moment.*

They'll never find us here.

Nash knew the first few conversations with Gabby would be critical, and he had rehearsed what he would say to her for months. She was starting to stir, so he put on a fresh pot of coffee. Then he placed a fresh icepack on the arm of the couch.

That lazy hillbilly Doyle had yet to accomplish anything in his life before he died, but at least he had a well-stocked houseboat. There was enough food, water, and supplies for Nash and Gabby to live on for weeks. Nash was hoping it wouldn't take that long to convince her.

"Where am I?" Gabby moaned. She tried to open one eye.

"You're safe," Nash replied.

"What have you done with me?" Gabby coughed. Her voice was weak from lack of use over the past two days.

"Please, try to get up slowly. The drugs will wear off soon, I promise." Nash sat down on a chair next to the couch and faced Gabby. "Here is an icepack for your head. You hit it pretty hard."

Just play it cool, Nash. You can do this.

Gabby refused to take it. "What drugs did you give me?"

"They were harmless—just something to help you sleep and make your head feel better. Would you like some fresh coffee?"

"I don't want anything. I just want to go home."
Gabby refused to look him in the eyes. She lifted her hand to her head.

"How about just a small cup? The coffee will help you wake up and make you feel better, and maybe you can forget about that nasty bump on your head."

Gabby looked down and saw her left ankle was chained to the table next to couch.

"Don't worry," Nash said quickly. "I'll take it off for good, soon. For now, just let me know when you have to use the bathroom and I'll remove it temporarily for you."

"Where am I?"

"We can discuss everything later—for now, you need to get some food and coffee in you. Would you like some pasta or rice?"

"*Where am I?*" she repeated. "What have you done to me?"

"Hey, it's okay," he said, trying to be soothing. "We are in the middle of nowhere, but we are safe. All I have done is taken you on a little trip, but nobody has laid a finger on you. I promise. You gave that bump on your head to yourself when you tried to run me over with the RV."

Gabby curled her one free leg up into a ball and clutched it with her arms as she turned away from him. "What do you want from me?"

"Just to talk, is all." Sweat started to bead on Nash's face. He knew this conversation would be difficult. "But first, I would like you to feel better—so please eat and drink something."

"I'd rather die."

"Gabby—"

"Don't say my name," she cut him off. "Don't you dare say my name."

"Okay, I'm sorry." A mosquito bit Nash on the back of his neck. When he slapped it, Gabby startled. She tried to scoot farther away, but the chain prevented it.

"Sorry, Ga—," he stopped himself. "Sorry, miss. I didn't mean to cause you any pain or discomfort. My name is Declan Nash, but you can call me Dec."

"I'll call you the devil." Gabby looked out into the darkness.

Nash, you fool. You're blowing it.

He would try again later. "I'll give you some time to be by yourself," he said. "Please don't hesitate to ask me for anything. Food, water, bathroom breaks, blankets, or anything else. Just let me know."

Gabby didn't respond. She shut her eyes and her lower lip curled up under her teeth as she fought back tears.

Nash slowly stood up and walked to the back of the houseboat and entered the bedroom. He turned around and looked at Gabby one more time, then shut the door.

CHAPTER 6

Williston, North Dakota

Cooper recently read an article about how Walmart stores had one of the highest rates of crimes of any location in a city—more than bars, casinos, parks, or gas stations. Most placed the blame on poor clientele and overnight RV squatters. Because of this, more police stations had started embedding officers at local Walmarts, including the store in Williston. It was lucky for Cooper, since the ready presence of a police officer had kept Mustache from taking a swing at him with that crowbar. The officers had referred to the man as Frederick Nickels, and Cooper overheard one officer comment about Nickels being high on meth again.

Meth, thought Cooper. *That explains a lot.*

The sound of keys jingling reverberated down the hallway at the Williams County Correctional Center in downtown Williston.

"Cooper Smith?" asked an officer.

"Yes, that's me."

"You're up. It's time for your one phone call."

There was a backlog at the jail, and it took all day for Cooper to get processed. Tension and chatter filled the air, mostly involving the blizzard that was expected to strike later that night.

Cooper had explained to the officers how Nickels blindsided him in the parking lot and came after him with the crowbar. The officers questioned him intensively about the tomahawk, but Cooper explained it was his only means of self-defense. The officers promised to review the security cameras from Walmart and get back to him. They said they would try to get to it that night.

Fat chance. You're stuck here overnight.

Soojin answered on the first ring.

"Soojin, it's me."

"What number are you calling from?"

"It's a long story." Cooper cleared his throat.

"What happened?"

"Wellstone was hit in a Walmart parking lot this morning. The man who hit me got out of his truck and tried to club me with a crowbar. We were both arrested, and I'm in jail."

"Wait, what?" Soojin asked in disbelief. "Are you hurt?"

"No, I'm fine." Cooper shifted the phone receiver to the other ear. "Just glad the police were there in time so I didn't have to use my tomahawk on that guy. Or worse, have him use his crowbar on my head."

"But ... but, why did he attack you?" asked Soojin.

"I really don't know," said Cooper. "But it sounds like the guy was on drugs and has a history of altercations like this. It was a rough way to start the trip, that's for sure."

Soojin sighed. "I have bad news, too. I tried to book tonight's flight from MSP to Williston, but it was canceled because of the weather. They are saying it may be days before another flight is scheduled. I checked the road report and the interstates are scheduled to be shut down tonight, too. There is one more flight out to Bismarck, and that's my only chance to get out closer to help find—"

"Gabby," Cooper finished.

"Yes."

"Okay, here's what we can do. Once I'm cleared, I can talk to one of these officers about Gabby. I'll try to get some answers and updates. In the meantime, do you think you could reach out to some of Gabby's close friends or family members?"

"I've already tried to reach out to a few people, but they are all busy looking for her. I've been keeping up with the Facebook updates, but there isn't much to go on right now. All we know is she was kidnapped from the recreation center on Saturday night by two men, and driven away in an RV. Every day that goes by . . ." Soojin's voice trailed off.

"I know, we need to hurry—"

A knock on the door interrupted Cooper. "Wrap it up in there," an officer instructed.

"Hun, I have to get going. I'll hopefully be out of here by tomorrow morning, but in the meantime, stay positive. We are going to find Gabby."

"We have to."

***

Just outside of Williston, the proud home of Mark and Sydney Hanson stood perched on a hill. Mark had served as North Dakota's state senator from District One for thirty years. Sydney kept him grounded even as voices in Bismarck raised his name as a potential candidate for governor. They had lost their only son, James, as well as his wife, in a car accident sixteen years ago. Gabby, their only granddaughter, was nine at the time and had been staying at their home when the accident happened.

Mark and Sydney had raised Gabby like she was their own daughter, and the three of them shared a close-knit relationship. When Gabby expressed an interest in exploring politics in college, Mark made the introductions needed to set her up for a successful political career. One of his proudest moments came when she was elected to the Williston City Council. From there, he knew it was nothing but up for her.

Things were going well for their family until the day that Sydney went in to see the doctor after she experienced unexplained weight loss and severe abdominal pain. She was diagnosed with pancreatic cancer and given less than five years to live. That was three years ago, and the family was still trying to come to terms with Sydney's illness and the reality that pancreatic cancer took the lives of over ninety percent of its victims within five years. Sydney had already beat the odds by making it this far, and she tried to stay strong. But rounds of surgeries and chemotherapy left her weak and resting most of the time. She was starting to feel a little better as of late, and some of her energy seemed to be returning.

That was, until last Saturday night.

Deplorable savages, he thought. *I'd put one between the eyes of each of them in a heartbeat if I could.* Mark's blood pressure began to rise again as he ruminated on it.

It was getting late, and Mark had left the porch light on. Sydney's hands and eyes began to twitch after she learned the news. It was too much stress for her body to deal with. A constant stream of visitors had stopped by since local news outlets had broken the story, with endless calls and messages of support. With the upcoming storm approaching, Mark had told everyone involved in the search to go home and get some rest, but to continue to reach out to folks online in neighboring communities. All they needed was one clue that could help point to where Gabby was. Mark had already posted her picture all over North Dakota, including on billboards, flyers, and local television. Local, state, and federal law enforcement authorities had been in continual contact with Mark. They were working hard, but even they confessed things would slow down for at least the next day with the snowstorm.

Mark was exhausted, but he had to accept this meeting tonight if he was going to get extra state-level resources from Bismarck. Plus, he knew he couldn't go too far from home with Sydney in her condition. He wanted so badly to be out there looking for Gabby, but he would have to settle for having other people lead the search parties. A set of car lights made their way up the driveway. After the vehicle stopped, the driver walked briskly up to the front door where Mark was waiting.

"Hello, Nate. Come on in, thanks for swinging by tonight." Mark greeted Thompson with a handshake and patted him on the back as he welcomed him into his home.

"Mark, thanks for having me." Thompson shook his coat off and slipped out of his boots. "I hate to drop in like this after all that has happened."

"It's no problem—we just have to keep the volume down a bit, as Syd is in bed already."

Thompson lowered his voice. "Sure thing. How's Sydney handling all this? How's her health?"

Mark hung his head. "I have to admit she's not doing very well. This has all been a bit too much for her to handle."

Thompson slowly nodded. "Well, please pass on my regards to her—and let her know I'm praying for her."

Mark forced a smile. "Thanks, I'll let her know."

"I'll make it brief, for both our sakes. I don't want to get caught in this storm, and you need to get some rest, too."

"Looks like it will be a pretty nasty one—someone said maybe two feet of snow." Mark shook his head. "Please come sit down in the living room. Can I get you some coffee?"

"No, that's quite all right," said Thompson. "I won't be long."

The two men sat down on couches that faced each other in front of the fire sizzling in Mark's stone fireplace.

"I just wanted to let you know the governor and I are doing everything we can to mobilize additional officers and rescue crews to help find Gabby," said Thompson. "We are going to get her back soon."

"Syd and I sure do appreciate anything you can do for Gabby right now. The more help we have, the better chance we have of getting her back." Mark leaned back and fought a yawn as he rubbed his eyes. "Why did you insist on coming up from Bismarck to see me when you could have just told me this on the phone?"

"Well, for two reasons. I wanted to come back home to Williston to prep our house for the storm, and I also wanted to talk to you face to face about our agreement." Thompson looked away from Mark and gazed into the fire. "Now, before you say anything, just hear me out. You and I go way back—"

"Oh, for Pete's sake. What is all this about?"

"As I was saying, we go way back. We were both born and raised here in Williston, and we served together for many years at the capital on behalf of District One. We also made our little deal with the devil, and we want to make sure you aren't going to do anything rash with all that has transpired over the past few days."

"You've got to be kidding me. Gabby was kidnapped!" Mark's face burned red. "And by 'we' I assume you mean you and Rick. Do you think I am even thinking about that con job the two of you pulled on me?"

"Hey, calm down." Thompson held up his hands in surrender as he looked down the hall. "I thought you said Syd was sleeping. Look, we just wanted to make sure when you are talking to all these news outlets and authorities that you don't make any references to our special oil clients."

"The fact that you have the gall to come into my home to talk about this right now is despicable," Mark spat. "Do you think I care about your precious oil right now? Or how you and Rick padded your pockets with bribes any chance you could?"

"The oil *is* precious. It's as good as gold as far as I'm concerned. But don't forget that you looked the other way when we came to you in confidence about drilling on protected lands. We all benefited."

"You fool! It's not gold. It's black gold. As black and dark as your soul has turned these past few years. Look what it's done to you; I don't even recognize the man in front of me. Worse, look what it's done to Williston and our state. We used to be known as the Peace Garden State. What happened to that?"

"This is our 1849 California gold rush, and we have to take advantage of it," Thompson insisted. "We were a sleepy, farming flyover state before we figured out how to juice the Bakken."

"You know, I'm a lot older than you, and my parents heard the same thing during the first Bakken-crazed days back in the fifties. Then I heard the same thing about our last so-called oil boom in the eighties. What happened after those booms? Well, I think you know how both of those busts left our community in a world of hurt. It took us years to recover from those swings. We invested in infrastructure, schools, and shops, all to accommodate the out-of-state oil companies and workers. As soon as the oil dried up, they were gone in a millisecond."

"This time is different, and you know that. We have enough reserves in the Bakken to last at least six generations."

"You're right, it is different this time. This time, we got all the crime, sex, drugs, and problems that come with housing roughnecks in our backyard. This time, we are raping our land so bad that there might not be a North Dakota two generations from now, let alone six. This time, those bastards came and took my Gabby." Mark stood up, shaking with rage. "This time, you'll regret the day you let greed overcome compassion when you visited a grandfather in distress."

"Mark—"

"Get the hell out of my house."

***

Cooper was getting restless in his jail cell and couldn't imagine someone spending the rest of his life in one of these cages. The heater in the jail could not keep up with the falling temperatures outside, and he started to shiver. He should be out trying to help find Gabby. And he desperately needed a smoke.

At least I made it to the ripe old age of twenty-five before I was thrown in jail.

Cooper chuckled when he thought about what his father and brothers would say if they knew where he was right now. Cooper's father had retired after thirty years with the Duluth Police Department, and all three of his brothers followed in his footsteps by joining law enforcement. Even Cooper's younger sister was working on a degree in criminal justice.

He had always been the outsider when it came to his career interests, which led him to journalism.

Cooper was born and raised in Duluth, and up until he moved to Saint Paul last year he had spent his whole life in northern Minnesota. Although that upbringing had prepared him to deal with any amount of frigid cold weather, he wasn't sure it had prepared him for prison life. Cooper had been a decent high school athlete, and at six feet tall and 190 pounds he could pack a punch, if needed. Still, his reddish-brown hair and freckles from his Irish ancestry took away some of his intimidation factor. And his fully intact pearly white teeth and undamaged nose suggested he wasn't much of a brawler.

I need to get out of here soon.

A door suddenly opened and Cooper heard heavy footsteps approach. The young officer who came with them looked like a meat-and-potatoes farm boy. He towered over Cooper. He had brown hair with a neatly groomed beard— the kind that wouldn't fly at a major city's police department but was fine in western North Dakota. His badge read *Officer Fletcher*.

"Cooper Smith?"

"Yes, that's me."

"Come with me."

Cooper followed Fletcher down the hallway into a side office with a small desk that housed a computer, two chairs, walls full of file cabinets, and D.A.R.E drug-resistance posters on the wall.

"Have a seat."

"Thanks. Is everything all right?"

"We reviewed the video camera from the Walmart parking lot and determined you did not instigate the accident or the ensuing altercation."

"Am I free to go, then?"

"After you out process, yes. But there is a bad storm arriving soon. If you were released now, is there a warm place you can hunker down for the night?"

"Well, I had planned to go and stay at one of the local hotels, but I'm not sure if anything is available right now."

"I may have a better option for you. My wife and I rent out our basement on Airbnb to make some extra cash, but with this storm we haven't been able to fill it. We usually charge two-hundred dollars a night, but since it's last minute we would take one-hundred a night if you would agree to stay at least three nights."

"I feel like there is a catch."

"No catch—although we have a newborn baby boy who cries a little at night."

"That's not an issue," Cooper said. "What is your son's name?"

"Jacob. He was born last week."

"Congratulations. Okay, count me in. Lets get out of here."

Cooper rode shotgun in Fletcher's police car as they made their way out to his home. "As a police officer, I would think you would be more reserved about letting strangers stay in your home," said Cooper.

"Well, I usually make everyone send me additional information about themselves so I can run their names in our databases to make sure there aren't any criminals looking to do damage. I pulled your record, of course, but you seem clean enough as far as I'm concerned."

"That's reassuring."

"Plus, once our guests see the police car in the driveway, they tend to be on their best behavior."

"Yeah, I bet. Say, do you mind if I have a smoke in here?"

Fletcher looked over at Cooper. "Are you serious?"

"Just a quick one, I'll crack the window."

"No way, man. When we get home you can have a smoke by the back door of our house, if you can get a cigarette to light in this weather."

Cooper tapped the box of cigarettes in his hand, then put them back in his pocket. "Okay, you're the boss."

Snow had started falling, and wind was blowing it sideways across the road. Fletcher's wipers swept across the windshield as he gripped the steering wheel to keep the car steady against the rising wind.

After a brief period of silence, Cooper asked, "What's the latest on Gabby's disappearance?"

Fletcher was silent for a moment. "You're a reporter, right?"

"Yes, for Minnesota Public Radio."

"I'm sorry, I can't tell you anything. Sheriff's policy."

"I know her, pretty well, actually. She was a bridesmaid in our wedding this fall, and she is a close friend of my wife. Gabby is almost like a sister to her—they roomed together in college. We want to do everything we can to help find her."

"Oh, well that changes things." Fletcher paused and thought for another minute as he stared out at the snow blowing in front of him. "So, this is all off the record, okay?"

"Of course."

Fletcher took a deep breath and exhaled slowly. "Well, it's a shame, a real shame. She was such a beautiful girl. I went to high school with her. She was our class president. She was going to take her grandfather's senate seat one day, and then who knows after that."

"Why are you saying 'was'? Is she dead?"

"Sorry, no. Not that we know of. She could be anywhere, but it doesn't look good."

"Who took her?"

"So far as we know two out-of-towners took her. They were roughnecks, and we got their information from the ID cards they used to check in at the rec center. One guy, Brock Doyle, is from Louisiana and he's been known to raise hell up here for the better part of the past year. The other one is a fella named Declan Nash. He's from Texas and he's been here for two years. We don't have much paper on Nash, but we are looking into it. We know they both lived out on the same man camp just west of Williston."

"Have you questioned his coworkers and other men at the camp?"

"Listen, I know you know Gabby and all, but this is an active investigation and I can't get into too many of the details right now."

"What if I agreed to stay for a week at your place, at seventy-five dollars a night? Would that help you share anything else? And, by 'sharing,' I mean not information for my work, just updates on a personal level for my wife and me."

"Make it eighty-five a night, and you have a deal. I actually need to pay for the new crib I bought on credit last week. None of what I share with you goes in the press, it's just for you and your wife. I don't want to lose my job or anything."

"Okay, deal. Yeah, I hear kids are expensive—I don't envy you there."

"It's not the expense that is the killer, it's the lack of sleep." Fletcher yawned. "Hopefully you can sleep through it, though. All right, here we are."

Fletcher turned the police car off of the main road down a cul-de-sac and into a small driveway. The car's beams lit up a small, one-story home with a two-car garage.

"We can talk more when I get back home in the morning after my shift," said Fletcher. "The baby is already sleeping, and I messaged my wife Linda to let her know you will be downstairs." Fletcher handed Cooper a small house key. "Just go around to the back door and there is a separate entrance to the basement down a flight of stairs. Have your smoke, and then head down. Everything you need will be inside—just stay quiet and don't wake our son or my wife will kill you—"

"Make sure to add that warning on your Airbnb listing," Cooper quipped.

Fletcher smiled. "I'll come down and get you in the morning."

CHAPTER 7

Williston, North Dakota

Between the whistling winds of the blizzard and the baby screaming above him, Cooper hadn't slept a wink all night. He couldn't get any work done, either, because he didn't know the family's WiFi password. He also had no reception on his phone. He couldn't even go out and smoke because the wind was too fierce. He spent most of the night eating black licorice and rummaging around the Fletcher basement. He found old Garth Brooks, Alan Jackson, and Travis Tritt cassette tapes on a shelf, as well as a huge supply room that rivaled any Cooper had seen on the *Doomsday Preppers* show. It included a gun case, ammunition, liquor, canned soup, flashlights, and a lifetime supply of Dakotah Beard Oil.

Why would a guy add so much beard oil to his shelter supplies?

Cooper opened a bottle and put some oil on his scraggily reddish-brown beard. He had grown his beard out on his European vacation in preparation for the trip out to North Dakota, and it felt good to finally put some product on his dried-out facial hair. The scent carried a hint of tobacco, coffee, and black pepper. It was the highlight of his visit to Williston so far, and he made a mental note to ask Fletcher about buying a bottle off of him.

Cooper smirked. *At least there is some oil in the state that can be used for good.*

There were several small windows at the top of the basement walls that were connected to exterior window wells. Snow had piled into each of the wells and all Cooper could see was white. A clock on the wall showed it was half-past five in the morning. At 5:31, Fletcher bounded down the steps. Snowflakes flew off his hat and coat as he made his way into the basement's living room, where Cooper sat on the couch.

"Good morning, Officer Fletcher. How was your shift?"

"Morning. Please, call me Steve. The blizzard made the shift long, but despite the storm we actually made some small progress on Gabby's case."

"What'd you get?"

"Let's grab some coffee upstairs and I can tell you."

Cooper followed Fletcher upstairs to the kitchen, which was a small, cozy room with dark oak cabinets and a rooster décor.

"How did you sleep?" Fletcher asked.

"Well, you weren't kidding about losing sleep once there is a kid involved."

They both laughed. He made another mental note to make sure Soojin was still faithfully taking her birth control pills.

"As you can hear by the silence, they are finally sleeping, so try to keep it down." Fletcher started the coffeemaker.

"So, what's the latest with Gabby?"

"This is still off the record right?"

"Sure."

The two men stood hunched over the kitchen's center island. Fletcher was nearly whispering.

"Okay, there was one final flight that arrived at the Dickinson airport last night from Denver, right before the storm hit. One of the passengers had left his vehicle in the long-term parking lot, but when he got to his parking spot his car was gone. In its place was a smashed-up RV camper with no license plates. The passenger immediately notified airport security, which in turn called the local Dickinson PD. The PD gave us a call, and from the rec center surveillance video we were able to identify it as the likely RV used by Gabby's kidnappers. The RV was carefully moved inside a nearby hanger before the snowfall so they could inspect it overnight. I'm still waiting to hear back on the results of that, but we should know something soon. Things are moving pretty slow this morning, though. The storm closed all the major interstates in the area; it'll be a while before a legitimate forensics team can get out there. But at least we have the description of the stolen vehicle."

"What's the protocol for finding the stolen vehicle?" Cooper asked. "By now they could be anywhere in the continental United States."

"There was a nationwide bulletin put out over the wire early this morning on the car. It was a 2013 blue Ford Taurus sedan with North Dakota plates. If any authorities stop that vehicle and run a search it should trigger an alert. Same thing with any tolls, and other checkpoints we now are hoping to set up. If we can even get a single video hit from a gas station or rest stop we may be able to piece together a better search-and-rescue plan."

"Well, at least the stolen vehicle is a good starting point. Was there any video from the airport of the vehicle swap?"

Fletcher poured two cups of coffee and handed one to Cooper. He was glad Fletcher left his coffee black, just like God intended it to be consumed.

"Yes, but the kidnappers placed the RV between the security camera and the vehicle they stole, and they only used the opposite side door. They must have known exactly where the camera was, because they shielded their work well. We are going to ask Dickinson airport security for additional camera footage to see if we can get any shots of them in the vehicle as they were leaving."

Cooper took a long sip of the coffee. It wasn't a cappuccino in Italy, but it tasted quite good for farmhouse coffee. And he really needed the caffeine.

"Well, I certainly do appreciate the updates," said Cooper. "It means a lot. Now, I'd like to help out, perhaps go interview some of the kidnappers' coworkers or neighbors. Any word on the status of my Jeep?"

Fletcher shook his head as he turned to look outside at the snow. "Sorry, but I heard it's totaled. It was towed to a local mechanic's shop, but everything is closed down now. Not that it would matter, with all the major roads being closed off."

My poor Wellstone. May he rest in peace.

"Oh," said Fletcher. "I almost forgot. I was officially assigned the Gabby kidnapping case, so I'll be your main law enforcement point-of-contact in case you find anything out about Gabby or her kidnappers. Please call or email me with updates you may have." Fletcher handed Cooper his business card.

Cooper nodded and grabbed the card. He studied it in his hands, then put it in his pocket. Reaching for his wallet, he pulled out his own business card and handed it to Fletcher. "Likewise, if you have any more updates you can share with me that might help in our efforts to locate Gabby, I would greatly appreciate it."

Fletcher glanced at Cooper's card before putting it in his chest pocket. "I'll share what I can."

Cooper took another long sip of his coffee as he followed Fletcher's gaze out the window. The backyard was small, blanketed in a fresh white layer of snow. At the end of the yard was a garage with a snow-covered roof. Something at the base of the garage caught Cooper's eye—a small black tarp sticking up through the snow.

"Hey, what's under that tarp out there?"

"It's an old Arctic Cat snowmobile, or snowcat, as we call them. Might actually get to use it now."

"How does it run?"

"I haven't started it since last year, but it's always worked just fine."

"Would you be willing to rent it out to me for the week? At least then I can get around, and you can make a few extra bucks to boot."

Fletcher turned back to face Cooper. "You're from the Twin Cities, right? You know how to ride one of these things?"

"I live in Saint Paul now, but I grew up in northern Minnesota. It's practically a necessity to learn how to ride up there. In fact, I got my snowmobile license long before I could legally drive a car."

"Hmm . . ." Fletcher looked at Cooper, then back outside toward the garage. "Well, I have a decent supply of gas out in the shed in five-gallon containers. How about I rent the snowcat out to you for thirty-five dollars a day, plus the cost of whatever gasoline you use."

Of course this guy would have a supply of gasoline. You never know when the zombie apocalypse will strike.

"You drive a hard bargain, but I'll take it as long as you point me in the right direction of where the kidnappers lived and worked."

"Not a problem, I'll even throw in a set of hand warmers."

"Perfect. Say, before I go, can I use your phone to call my wife quick? I have zero reception with my cell out here. I also need to grab your WiFi password if that's all right with you."

"Phone's around the corner, just talk softly and make sure she doesn't call the house number when the kid is sleeping. I'll write you the WiFi password quick and then I'll head out and get the snowcat ready while you're on the phone."

"Talk about service—I'll make sure to give you a great recommendation on Airbnb at the end of my stay."

"You bet."

Cooper found the phone up on the hallway wall; it was an old landline with a long connected cord that dangled down on the ground. Cooper picked it up and dialed Soojin's cell.

"Where have you been?" Soojin demanded when she heard his voice. "Are you still in jail?"

"I actually got out last night and I'm staying at one of the officer's houses. It's like an Airbnb-type arrangement," he said. "I have absolutely no phone reception out here. Where are you?"

"Why are you whispering?" Soojin asked.

"Hah. Just remind me to tell you later about baby sleep patterns in the first week of life."

"Oh jeez, I can't think about that right now."

"Were you able to get in last night?"

"Yeah, I made the last flight into Bismarck around 9:30 pm. That's the closest I could get with the storm approaching. I have a rental car, but with all the roads being closed I'm as good as stuck at a hotel here."

"I'm glad you made it in safely. What's the latest you've heard on Gabby?"

"Not much. I plan to call her grandfather soon to see how I can help, and then make my way up there as quickly as I can. What have you heard?"

Cooper filled Soojin in on the latest from Fletcher about the stolen vehicle at the airport in Dickinson, and the bulletin out on the car.

"You might be better off staying down there or getting to Dickinson to see if you can get any more answers," said Cooper.

"What's your plan?"

Just then Cooper heard a low rumble outside. He stretched the phone cord down the hallway and peaked out the kitchen window. Fletcher had the snowcat running and it was sitting in the middle of his backyard.

"I'm going to go out and see if I can interview some people. I'll be on email later today and will let you know what I find out."

"Okay. Be careful, and don't end up in jail again."

"I'll try my best."

***

It had been a few years since Cooper had driven a snowmobile, but for someone from Minnesota, it was like riding a bike. Cooper raced the snowcat across an open field. The snow was fresh and deep, and the machine handled well.

The man camp wasn't far, just north of Williston on Highway 2. Following Fletcher's directions, Cooper quickly found a main road that would lead him straight to it. There was no traffic, save for a snowplow making its way toward him from the opposite side of the road. Oil drills lined the road on either side. Most of the drilling platforms were miraculously plowed out already, the drills gyrating into the earth. Gas flares burned off the excess flammable material, and the flames created a mirage effect as they shimmered over the white blanket of snow.

A large sign with the picture of his beloved Paul Bunyan stood at the outer edge of the man camp. Cooper stopped his snowcat and lifted the visor on his helmet for a closer look. Instead of holding his customary double-bladed axe, Paul was holding an oil drill with one hand and giving a thumbs-up with the other as he flashed a cheesy smile.

Come on, North Dakota, Cooper thought. *Stealing our iconic folklore legend is a bit of a low blow.*

Next to the picture of Paul Bunyan read the words:

Paul Bunyan's Band of Oilmen: Lodging for the Working Man

Rates from $100 a night
Best Amenities and Food in Town

Cooper flipped his visor back down and rode into the camp. As he entered, he saw a sign pointing in three directions—RV and truck parking to the left, dormitory spaces to the right, and the main lobby and cafeteria straight ahead. Cooper thought about visiting the cafeteria first so he could talk to several people at once, but it was still early and the building looked dark. Cooper turned left. He rounded a huge snow mound left by a snowplow, then turned down a line of RVs. The RVs were stacked closely together, with snow filling the space between them.

A few pickup trucks were intermingled with the RVs, and one caught Cooper's eye. The truck was still covered in snow, but a bright red light glowed from the dash. Cooper made his way over to it. When he neared the truck he could see the light was coming from a space heater. Cooper turned off the snowcat and took off his helmet. He walked up to the truck and saw the space heater was pointed at a man who was reclined in the passenger side front seat. Music blared from the man's radio as Cooper walked up to the window and tapped against it lightly with his glove.

The man casually turned and cracked the door open. "Whaddya need?"

"Can we chat quick? I have a couple questions for you."

"Sure." The man nodded toward the driver's side seat. Cooper walked around to the driver's side door and slid in.

"Hey, I'm Cooper."

"I'm Sawyer. Nice to meet you."

The men shook hands with their gloves on. Sawyer wore a red and black winter bomber hat with built-in flaps to keep the beard and chin warm. He had buttoned the flaps on top of his head. It was difficult to tell his size as his outfit resembled Randy's triple-layer snowsuit in the *A Christmas*

Story movie. He looked to be in his thirties, with a scruffy beard and grease on his face and neck. After they shook hands the two men turned to sit shoulder-to-shoulder as they looked outside the front window.

"You live in this truck?" asked Cooper.

"Yeah. It's not much but it's cheaper than getting a room in the dorms. That means more cash for my family back home."

"Would you like a smoke?" Cooper took off his glove and handed his box of cigarettes to Sawyer, one already poking out the top.

"Sure, thanks." Sawyer took it out and Cooper handed him a lighter. Sawyer lit it and took a long pull, then handed the lighter back to Cooper.

"You mind if I join you?" asked Cooper.

"Go right ahead."

"You want me to crack my window?"

"Nah, just let it linger—it'll be warmer that way," said Sawyer.

Cooper took a long inhale, and then blew the smoke out of the corner of his mouth away from Sawyer. "So, where's home?"

"Are you like a reporter, or what?" Sawyer turned to look Cooper over.

Cooper turned in kind. "Sorry. Yes, I'm a reporter with Minnesota Public Radio. I actually have a few questions about a couple guys that live in this camp."

"I thought you were a reporter. I've talked to a few, you know. Even a reporter from the New York bloody-Times. You think I'd ever be talking to a *New York Times* reporter down in Alabama?"

"So, you're from Alabama. How long have you been up here?"

"Three years now. Three long, hard, and incredibly lonely years. Truth is, I'll talk to any reporter who stops by, just for some company. I see my family once a year, usually around Christmas. This year I had to cancel because things look like they may slow up a bit in 2015. I have to get while the gettin's good. You know what I mean?"

"What family did you leave behind back home?"

"My wife, and our two children. The kids are in school now, so I'm not missed too much. I'd like to get back down there though once I can get enough money."

"How much is enough?"

"I have a lot of debt. Too much. I made a lot of bad investments back in 2006. Times were good then. When the economy went belly-up in 2008 I ran up so much debt I couldn't even pay my rent. This—" Sawyer raised his hands outward as if spanning them across the Bakken. "This oil has given me a chance to get back to even."

"If you don't mind me asking, how much can you make in a month?"

"Good months we'll rake in around six to seven thousand dollars. I send most of the money home. If I didn't, I'd spend it all on booze and gambling like some of the other guys."

"Where do you shower?"

"Well, I usually shower here in the camp, but the showers are disgusting. I mean they're absolutely filthy." Sawyer wrinkled his nose. "So, sometimes I head down to the rec center, because their showers are much hotter and cleaner."

Cooper motioned toward the dorms. "What's it like in there?"

Sawyer shrugged. "There is a huge cafeteria in there, lined with video games and televisions. They should be opening for breakfast soon, so you can take a look around and order some flapjacks and bacon if you're hungry. I go in there sometimes when I'm bored. There are long hallways with bare white walls, and huge numbers hanging down from the ceiling so the guests know what wing they are in. The rooms are tiny, about half the size of a normal college dorm room.

"And you wouldn't believe what they charge," Sawyer continued. "It's three to four thousand a month, depending on demand. For that much, what's the point of even being up here?"

Cooper blinked in surprise. Fletcher's Airbnb basement room was suddenly looking pretty affordable.

"Do you mind if I ask you a few questions about a couple of the men from this camp?" Cooper said, changing the subject.

"Sure, who are you interested in?"

Cooper instinctively reached for his coat pocket to grab a pen and small notepad, then stopped himself. He thought it would be better to try to get a general feel for things before he went into full-on reporter mode. "A couple of guys named Nash and Doyle. I don't know if you heard, but they're suspects in the kidnapping of a city councilwoman this past weekend."

Sawyer nodded. "I did hear about that. It's been the talk of the camp."

"Did you know either of them?"

"Not personally, although I've seen them around a little. Your best bet is to talk to Marshall in the RV next door. He's a pretty cool dude from Texas. He even lets me come over and watch my Alabama Roll Tide football team on his DirecTV sometimes."

"Thanks for the tip. You want me to get you anything? It can't be fun to be confined in a truck all the time."

"Nah, I'm good. It's definitely not fun, but it could be worse. Plus, one day I'll be debt-free, and my sons can go to college. Maybe then they'll all be proud of me and how I sacrificed to better our family."

"I'm sure they will be."

Cooper shook Sawyer's hand and exited the vehicle. Flicking his cigarette to the ground, he walked around to the RV parked right next to Sawyer's truck. He knocked on the door, and a large black man answered. He was wearing a blue and black flannel shirt, blue jeans, and slippers. He had a short, trimmed beard and wore glasses.

"Can I help you?"

"Yes, I'm looking for Marshall."

"Who sent you?"

Cooper turned and pointed toward Sawyer. Sawyer waved from his truck.

Marshall sarcastically waved back like they were neighbors living in their suburban houses in Pleasantville. "Okay, come on in, but take your boots and coat off so you don't get snow everywhere."

"Great, thanks. My name is Cooper, and I'm a reporter from Minnesota Public Radio."

"Nice to meet you, radio man. Please feel right at home, just don't touch anything." Marshall winked.

Marshall's RV was impeccably clean—it could have been a showroom model for any RV dealership in America. It was neatly decorated with brown furniture and blue drapes and rugs. A flat-screen television blared ESPN from the corner. Marshall turned down the volume and looked back at Cooper.

"Would you like a beer?"

"Sure. Nice place you got here. I wasn't expecting it to be so . . ."

"Clean? Yeah, I get a lot jokes from the guys because of it, but what can I say? I like things in order. Guess it's my old military habits. Have a seat over here in the kitchen." Marshall gestured to the bench seat on the far end of the table.

"Which branch were you in?"

"Army. Did two tours in Iraq and that was enough for me."

Marshall dug a beer out of his smartly arranged refrigerator and handed it to Cooper.

"Thanks." Cooper looked down at it and saw it was a can of Natural Ice beer. "Wow, Natty Ice. I haven't had this stuff since college."

"Yeah, it's cheap as hell but it does the trick. It's all I'm willing to pay for on my tight budget. Want a koozie?"

"No thanks. Would you mind telling me a little bit about yourself? How long have you been living up here in this RV?"

Marshall cracked open a beer and sat down across from Cooper. "Well, I got out of the military in 2009. Came back home to Texas and the economy had collapsed. I mean, it absolutely just fell apart. I did some odd jobs for a couple years, but it wasn't enough. I heard some guys talk about all the money being made up here in Dakota, so I jumped at the opportunity. Been here three full years now."

"You ever miss home?"

Marshall shook his head. "My dad's been on me ever since I got out of the military about getting a real job and doing something with my life. You ever feel like you don't live up to your family's expectations?"

Cooper nodded. "Yeah, my whole family is in law enforcement. My dad really wanted me to join the police profession, but I became a reporter. Imagine the angst that caused my old man."

"Yeah, I bet. My dad also wanted me to join the local police. I just couldn't do it, though. I am done with guns."

"I hear you." Cooper grabbed a bag of licorice out of his pocket and held it up for Marshall. "Want one?"

"Black licorice?" Marshall shot him a look of disgust. "Nah, that stuff's nasty."

Cooper laughed. "That's what my wife says. Say, what do you do for fun around here?"

Marshall pointed at his TV. "I have DirecTV set up. What more could a guy ask for? Well, a winning season for the Cowboys would be nice once in a while. That's not going to happen until we get rid of Romo. Talk about a wasted 'franchise quarterback.'" Marshall signed air quotations with his hands.

"I'm a lifelong Vikings fan, so I feel your pain. At least your franchise has won a few Super Bowls—we are oh-for-four."

"The Purple People Eaters. My father used to rave about that defense. The glory years."

"The glory years, indeed. I'll drink to that." Cooper bumped his can against Marshall's and took a long drink of the Natty Ice. "Mmm, still tastes like piss."

Marshall let out a boom of a laugh as Natty Ice shot out of his nose. Cooper responded with the same, and soon the table was full of beer. Marshall regained his composure and with military precision quickly grabbed Clorox disinfectant wipes. He scrubbed down the table and dried it off with paper towels.

Cooper couldn't hold back a smile. "I don't want to take up too much of your time, but I actually came to see if you knew anything about a couple of guys that live at this camp. Their names are Nash and Doyle."

Marshall threw the wipes away and sat back down. "Sure, I know those guys, a little bit. What do you want to know?"

Cooper took out a notepad from his inside coat pocket. "Well, I'm sure you heard about the kidnapping last weekend, so I had a few questions related to that."

Marshall took a sip of his beer. "Yeah, I really can't believe it. Well, I mean I could see Doyle doing something like that, but not Nash."

"What do you mean by that?"

"The thing is, Doyle's an idiot, right? I mean, a pure idiot straight out of the Louisiana bayou. But he is tough as nails and is known to abuse women. Well, I mean it could just be camp rumors, but I've heard from other guys that

Doyle has bragged about being rough with prostitutes. And most of his 'dates' end in someone calling 911 on him." Marshall made air quotes when he said the word *dates*. "That girl they kidnapped was pretty good looking, so I could see Doyle doing something stupid like that. But Nash, no, not him." Marshall shook his head. "Nash was a private guy. I guess you could even call him shy. I talked to him a little bit because we were both from Texas. He was a Ranger down there."

"Like the baseball team, or like Chuck Norris?"

"Like Walker Texas Ranger. He didn't talk about it a lot, and I never did figure out how he went from doing that to doing this. Something must have happened. Either way, it doesn't make sense that he would kidnap that girl. Again, I don't know him real well, but that's just the read I have on him."

"Anything else strike you about him?"

"Funny you should ask." Marshall leaned back and put his hands behind his head. "I think one of the main reasons he and I got along was we are both very similar in regards to our obsessive natures."

"How so?"

"Well, people joke I have OCD, but the few people that know anything about Nash know he was *really* OCD. But not like cleaning and keeping things in order. He had some strange things he would obsess over. He'd make these lists, these dumb little lists of words. He would make them right in front of me. They always had to be seven-word lists. It kind of drove me nuts."

"What kind of lists?"

"Oh, anything really. I'd have a Cowboys football game on and he would make a list of seven phrases that described the Cowboys' new billion-dollar stadium, or he would have a list about Williston. It went on and on."

"Any other obsessive behaviors?"

"Yeah, he always had to sleep in the same dorm room, and have the same meals every day. He had his routines and things that had to be exact. But, like I said, he didn't share too much with me about anything else. Our interactions were limited to Texas, oil, and the weather."

"Where in Texas is he from?"

"Amarillo. He grew up on a cattle farm there."

Cooper scribbled on his notepad. "Do you know if anyone else was close to Doyle or Nash here in the camp or the city?"

Marshall thought about it for a minute. "You know, yeah, there was a third guy that hung around those two. I think his name is Nickels. Yeah, that's it, Nickels. I think he may actually be locked up at the jail, though. He had another run-in with the police."

Unbelievable. Nickels, really? Just my luck.

"This Nickels guy, what does he look like?"

"You can't miss him—he wears this ridiculously thick mustache. It's so big it would put even Tom Selleck to shame."

Cooper shook his head.

"What, you know the guy?" asked Marshall.

"Yeah, I met him the other day, seems like a bit of a hothead."

"You got that right."

Cooper inwardly cringed at the thought of another encounter with Nickels, but he forced himself to ask, "When he's not in jail, where can I find him?"

"He stays in the dorms here, so you could look there. Otherwise, I know he likes to go out and drink at the bars downtown. Either way, he'll know the most about Nash and Doyle, may even know where they are hiding."

Cooper finished off the rest of his beer. "Well, Marshall. Thanks for the hospitality and for chitchatting. Maybe I'll have to stop back and watch a Cowboys game with you sometime."

"You're welcome back anytime, radio man. Just bring your own beer next time."

"You know I will."

CHAPTER 8

Bismarck, North Dakota

The Patterson Hotel in downtown Bismarck had been a hotspot in North Dakota since it was first built in the early nineteen-hundreds. The ten-story building was notorious during prohibition for serving alcohol, hosting illegal gambling, and housing prostitutes. Several presidents had stayed there, including Theodore Roosevelt and John F. Kennedy. Some even circulated rumors that JFK snuck girls into his Patterson hotel room via a secret underground tunnel from the train station across the street. Its main lobby now served as the Peacock Alley American Grill and Bar, a local gathering place for politicians and lobbyists.

The night after the blizzard, Governor Simmons called the owner of Peacock Alley and asked him to prepare the Langer Room. Simmons said he had an important meeting that he didn't want to take at his home, and he insisted on using the restaurant's private back room. Simmons went straight there and stopped to smirk up at the picture of William Langer, one of North Dakota's most colorful politicians who served as both the seventeenth and twenty-first governor of the state.

Trent Wheeler, a private investigator who had retired from the North Dakota Highway Patrol after thirty years of service, was already waiting for him. He knew every square inch of the state and had dirt on everyone from Simmons all the way down to the newest state capitol intern. He wore his hair cut short and neat and remained clean-shaven, as if he would be ready to report for the state patrol academy tomorrow. Wheeler's steely blue eyes had the power to stop a criminal in his tracks, and they locked on Simmons as he approached to shake his hand.

"Governor Simmons, it's nice to see you again." Wheeler gave his signature vice-grip handshake.

"Good to see you, too, Trent. Easy on the hand." Simmons shook his crushed hand out as he forced a smile.

"Why the rush to meet? I had to take my truck with the attached snow plow just to cut a path here tonight."

You'll meet when I ask you to meet. Simmons smiled and sat down across from Wheeler. "Yeah, thanks for coming on such short notice. Let's eat and have a drink and then we can talk business."

Wheeler eyed the door. "With all due respect, I'd rather just talk and get out of here so we aren't seen together. Why didn't you just have me come to your house?"

Simmons sat back and took a cigar and lighter out of his pocket. "You mind?"

He shook his head.

The cigar end was already cut, and Simmons lit it and took the first few puffs to get it going. Then he set it on an ashtray and looked up at Wheeler. "You know how it is, security has been a little tighter at the house as of late, and all of my guests are being checked into an official public record document. Those intrepid Democrats insisted on the policy last year. The media caught on, and now I have to submit all of my guests to the capitol." Simmons shook his head. "As if those donkeys don't have anything better to worry about."

"Let's just cut to the chase. What do you need from me?"

"I assume you've heard about the kidnapping of Senator Hanson's granddaughter last weekend up in Williston."

"Yes, of course. Who hasn't?"

"Right, so I have a job for you. I want you to go offer your services to Senator Hanson. Tell him you want to help find Gabby."

Wheeler eyed Simmons up and down. "Why would you pay for that? I thought you couldn't stand the guy."

What is with this guy's eyes? Simmons picked up his cigar and took a long pull from it. "You're right, I can't stand him or his granddaughter. Between us, I'm glad she is gone. But the problem is, Hanson is out of his mind right now. I think he may lose his cool and do something irrational."

"You mean he'll talk about the bribes and the protected lands?"

"Come on man, keep it down." Simmons tapped ashes off his cigar. "But yes. I don't want all of us going down over this guy."

"Why don't you just send Thompson up to talk to him, set him straight."

Simmons put his cigar down. "That's the problem—I did. Thompson went and talked to him and Hanson is worse now than I thought. He is a loose cannon."

Wheeler leaned forward in his chair. "So, you want me to keep tabs on him. See who he talks to, and make sure he doesn't share anything sensitive about your arrangement?"

"Exactly. Go tell him you'll help out with Gabby, and be there lock-in-step with him at his house or wherever he goes. Tell him you'll help on a *pro bono* basis."

"I'm not that close to him; he probably wouldn't think it's genuine."

"Okay, fine. Tell him you'll work for free until Gabby is safely returned. At that point you can ask for him to pay your fee. I assume a distressed grandparent would go for that."

Wheeler grinned. "It's worked for me before."

"See. All right, that's perfect." Simmons impulsively flashed a thumbs up. "Try to shield the media as best you can, and if anyone gets close, let me know and we can deal with them."

"Sure."

Simmons eyed Wheeler. "The usual amount?"

Wheeler stared him down in response. "Yeah, plus a bonus if I keep Hanson in check until this thing all blows over."

Not one to back down, Simmons pointed his cigar at Wheeler. "That can be arranged—but remember, your ass is on the line here, too. You know about our little ponzi scheme, so your incentive should be as great as ours to get this guy."

Wheeler smiled. "The biggest difference is I have so much dirt on you and Thompson, that you can't touch me. Plus, I covered my tracks better than you both. Just pay me for my services, and we'll all be fine."

"All right, deal, tough guy." Simmons raised a hand in mock defense. "Just keep Hanson in check."

"Don't worry, I will."

"Are you sure you don't want to stay for a drink?"

Wheeler stood up and motioned for Simmons to stay seated. "Have a good night, governor. I'll be in touch."

CHAPTER 9

The Louisiana Bayou

Gabby was getting restless as she lay on the uncomfortable couch, her leg shackled to a table. The drugs were finally wearing off. She had no idea what day it was, or how long it had been since she was first taken. Even the events of that night were foggy. One thing she knew for sure was that she hadn't been raped or physically abused—she would have felt that in her body. She was thankful for that, but she wondered if he had touched her or even kissed her while she was out. She shuddered.

"I know what you're thinking," said Nash. "But don't worry, no one has touched you, except when I moved you to a new location."

Jeez, can this guy read my mind? Gabby thought.

She suddenly recalled Nash hitting Bulldog across the head and burying him in front of her. She clenched her hands at the thought of it, and out of the corner of her eye she could see him staring at her. A candle on the table in front of him silhouetted his body upon the wall.

"Did you really kill your partner with a pickaxe?" Gabby asked.

Nash slowly crossed his arms and looked away from her. "He was a nobody, a Louisiana redneck just looking to make a few bucks and raise some hell up in North Dakota. The world is a better place without him."

And it would be a better place without you. Gabby turned completely away from Nash.

"Want to help me make a list?" asked Nash. "I am trying to come up with seven things that describe North Dakota. Want to join in?"

Gabby lay silent, refusing to acknowledge him.

"Okay, suit yourself. This is what I have so far."

NORTH DAKOTA:
1. *Monotonous Slave Labor*
2. *Frozen Tundra*
3. *Country Folk*
4. *Pillaged Land (The oil brought me cash and you)*
5. *Lonesome Territory (That is until I thankfully found you)*
6.
7.

"Since those first five words are a little negative, would you object if I use your first and last name for number six and seven?"

Gabby had had enough. She needed some answers, and she needed them now.

"Why did you take me?"

Nash was silent for a moment. "Well," he finally said, "that's a difficult question to answer."

"No, it's not."

Nash paused again, then looked up at Gabby. "I first saw your picture in the newspaper, and I was immediately struck by how beautiful you were. I had never seen anyone like you, and quite frankly, you were the type of woman I always dreamed of being with. Then I heard you give an interview to a local news network. You were so well spoken, and I could tell you were raised well. I was absolutely smitten."

Unbelievable. This guy had a crush on me?

"Why didn't you just approach me and ask me out for coffee like a normal person?" Gabby looked in the direction of Nash to gauge his reaction.

"I, well . . ." he stuttered.

Gabby felt a glimmer of hope for the first time. *This guy doesn't want to hurt me,* she realized. *He wants me to love him.*

"It's not like you are a terrible-looking guy, and you look like you are my age. Why not just ask me on a date?"

Nash squirmed in his chair.

"Well, I wanted to. I really did, but I read in the newspaper all the negative things you were saying about us roughnecks. Then I went to one of your city council meetings, and sat in the back to listen and see you in person. You were talking about trying to clean up some of the man camps including the one I was in." Nash's voice was shaky.

Gabby looked Nash directly in his eyes. "So, instead you decided to kidnap me, kill your partner, and drag me out to the middle of a swamp? Did you really think that was going to win me over?"

"Listen, Gab—"

"Don't you dare call me that; we are not on a first-name basis."

Nash hung his head and slumped down in his chair. No one spoke. After several minutes, he slowly stood and lumbered toward the door to the outside. Pulling it open, he stopped in the doorframe. He looked back at Gabby.

"You will be free," he said. "But I'm afraid I can't let you go right now." He walked outside and closed the door behind him.

Gabby turned away from the door and smiled to herself. *I'm not going to die.*

CHAPTER 10

Williston, North Dakota

The fallout from the blizzard had finally passed; cars zipped along the interstates again, the only sign of the recent storm were the snowdrifts lining the sides of the road and the patches of ice and frost on the roads' surfaces. Soojin didn't have much luck getting answers about Gabby's disappearance in Bismarck or Dickinson, so she made her way up to Williston.

Cooper was in the Fletcher home's entryway updating Fletcher on what he had discovered at the man camp. When Cooper saw Soojin pull up into the driveway, he shook Fletcher's hand and said goodbye. She picked him up in her green Subaru Forester crossover rental car. Their next stop was the Hanson residence.

"Nice ride." Cooper hopped in the passenger seat and closed the door. "All-wheel drive, right?"

"Yeah, I was going to just pick up an economy-sized car, but I figured the extra size and traction would be good in this weather." Soojin backed out of the driveway and pulled out onto the highway.

"Good idea. So, why do you think Senator Hanson wants to speak with me?" Cooper asked.

"When I called him on the phone yesterday he asked that both of us come see him. Then he just mentioned he also wanted to speak with you about a private matter," said Soojin. "That was all he said, so I have no idea."

"I'm curious about it." Cooper looked out the window as they passed the oil drills that lined the highway. "Hopefully it's good news about Gabby."

"I think we could all use a bit of that today."

Cooper took a bag of licorice out of his jacket pocket and held it up for Soojin.

"You're still eating that crap?"

"You bet. I brought ten bags of it with me for this trip alone. It's an acquired taste, I'll admit, but it's so good once you acquire it."

Soojin rolled her eyes.

"Hey, do you know what I just realized?" asked Cooper.

"What's that?"

"You're going to miss your Taekwondo tournament this weekend back in Minneapolis."

"Yeah, I know." Soojin slowed down the car as she encountered a stalled line of semi-trucks. "They'll be more tournaments; my time is better served looking for Gabby. Plus, I wouldn't be able to focus while she is still missing."

Cooper looked over at Soojin and marveled at the fact that his new wife was a fourth degree black belt in Taekwondo.

"How many more years before you become a fifth degree?"

"Should be about two years as long as I keep after it."

"Your mother would be really proud; I know she is looking down from heaven and smiling at you and your accomplishments."

"Now's not the time to get sentimental, Cooper—we have a mission to accomplish." Soojin shot Cooper one of her killer stares. Like she was sizing up an opponent before a match.

"Okay, okay." Cooper put his hands up in defense. "Well, I'm proud of you, too, and don't you forget it. Say, is Governor Knutson cool with you taking all this time off? I know you missed a lot work while we were on our honeymoon."

"He told me to take as much time as I need. He knows of Senator Hanson and his reputation, and he was supportive of my trip out here."

"That's good."

"We're here," said Soojin. She turned the car into the Hanson driveway and parked it in front of the garage. A black Dodge Charger was parked in the driveway as well.

"I wonder who else is here." Cooper put one more piece of licorice in his mouth before he closed up the bag and put it in his pocket.

"Guess we'll find out."

Just as Soojin raised her hand to knock on the front door, Senator Mark Hanson opened it.

"Hello, Soojin! It's been too long." Soojin gave Mark a big hug. "And this must be your husband, Cooper. Please come on in." Cooper shook Mark's hand.

"It's been far too long, Senator Hanson," said Soojin. "I remember that last trip I had out here with Gabby during one of our university's winter breaks. I thoroughly enjoyed my time with you and Mrs. Hanson."

"Then you'll remember you have to call me Mark, and my wife, Sydney. None of this formal nonsense."

"It's a pleasure meeting you," said Cooper. "I'm so sorry to hear about Gabby. I hope we can find her soon."

"Me too, young man. We might have some more help. Come into the living room—I want you to meet someone."

As they entered the living room, a man stood up from the couch and turned to greet them.

"This here is Trent Wheeler. He's a private investigator and he knows this state better than any flickertail that roams the land. With his help we may just be able to get Gabby back."

Wheeler shook hands with Cooper and Soojin, his vice-grip taking Cooper by surprise.

"Nice to meet you both," said Wheeler. "How do you two know Gabby?"

"I was her roommate in college," said Soojin. "She was one of my bridesmaids at our wedding. I'm glad you are here to help get her back."

"I'll certainly do everything in my power to find her."

"Soojin works for Minnesota's governor, and Cooper is a reporter for Minnesota Public Radio," said Mark. "So, they have some good connections across the border in case you find something there."

"Good to know," said Wheeler. "What did you say your last name was?"

"Smith. Cooper Smith."

"Thanks, I may just call on you. Here's my card." Wheeler handed a business card to Cooper.

Cooper took it and looked it over.

Trent Wheeler
Private Eye
Retired North Dakota State Trooper

"Thanks," said Cooper. He fished out his own card and handed it over to Wheeler. "Feel free to call me anytime—that's my cell phone on the card."

"Perfect, I'll do that."

"Okay, Trent," said Mark. "I don't want to keep you here any longer. Please let me know if you find anything at all about Gabby. Call me day or night."

Wheeler went to shake Mark's hand, but Mark pulled back. "I think one handshake from you is enough," he chuckled.

Wheeler smiled. "I'll talk to you soon."

Mark walked Wheeler out toward the front door, and Cooper and Soojin looked at each other.

"A private eye?" Cooper whispered. "What do you think of that?"

"Well, if it gives us a better shot at finding Gabby, I'm all for it," said Soojin.

The front door slammed shut and Mark came back to the living room.

"Where's Sydney? How is her health?" asked Soojin.

"She is resting in the bedroom," said Mark. "She isn't doing too well right now; please keep her in your prayers."

Soojin placed her hand over her mouth. "I'm so sorry to hear that."

"We will certainly keep your whole family in our prayers," said Cooper.

"That would be great," said Mark. "Please, have a seat. Can I get you guys some tea or coffee?"

"No, I'm okay," said Soojin.

"I'm fine," said Cooper. "You have a lovely home— nice and cozy."

"Thank you," said Mark. "We sure are proud of it."

An intercom system buzzed behind Mark. He reached for it and turned up the volume.

"Do you need anything, honey?" asked Mark.

Sydney spoke softly. "Are the Smiths here?"

Mark pushed the button on the intercom to respond. "Yes, they just arrived." "Could you just have Soojin come down the hall so I can say hello?" she asked.

Mark looked up at Soojin, who nodded as she stood up.

"She'll be right down." Mark let go of the intercom button and turned back around to face Soojin and Cooper.

"It's the last door on the left." Mark pointed in the direction of the hallway.

Soojin smiled and left the room, and Mark sat down across from Cooper.

"Cooper, thanks again for coming over and for offering to help."

"It's my pleasure. I was actually already in town working on a story about the oil boom. But to my editor's chagrin, I've put the story on hold until we can find Gabby."

"That's what I wanted to talk to you about. Soojin mentioned on the phone yesterday that you were here for work." Mark leaned forward. "I've wanted to talk to the media for a long time about something very important to me. I don't want to talk to some national-level media, and I certainly don't want to talk to any local media. I've wanted to talk to someone I can trust. Someone I know will tell a story exactly how it happened, without any connections to the industry."

"Are you talking about the oil industry?"

"Yes." Mark shook his head. "That wretched three-letter word has brought me so much misery."

"Well, I'm more than happy to see what I can do for you. Is this about Gabby?" Cooper grabbed his notepad and pen.

"There's no need for that yet." Mark motioned toward Cooper's notepad. "I did some research and placed some calls about you yesterday. I know what kind of person you are, and the work you've done. That story you did on the heroin network, and how you helped to take down the drug dealers was some pretty serious stuff. What was your series called again?"

"*Brown Sugar in Minnesota,* but don't hype my role up too much. It was the law enforcement officers who brought down the dealers."

"Don't be so humble. Anyway, I know you and Soojin, and I know you can help get Gabby back."

"What about that private investigator?"

"He knows North Dakota. Knows it better than anyone else in the state, but that's just it. I don't think Gabby is in North Dakota anymore. There's no way those roughnecks stayed in the state to hunker down. My guess is they are somewhere down south hiding out with Gabby. I need you and Soojin to go find them and Gabby. When you do, bring her back to me and I'll give you a story that will make headlines around the country."

Well that would sure get Wild Bill's heart pumping. And mine, too.

"Gee, senator, I appreciate the offer, but—"

"Don't say any more. I know you didn't offer to help find Gabby because you wanted anything in return. I'm telling you that when you bring Gabby back, I will have a story for you. And, call me Mark, please."

Cooper tapped his thumbs together. "Can you give me a little bit more on what your story might entail? If I'm going to get more resources from my editor, I'll need to give him something more."

Mark looked away from Cooper out the window. "I can't say too much right now, because I'm unfortunately caught up in the middle of it all. But I can say it involves corruption and blackmail, and when all the parties are exposed it will rattle our dear state to its core. More than it already has been by all this drilling."

Cooper waited to see if Mark would say anything else, but he didn't. "Are you in trouble, senator?" Cooper shook his head. "I mean Mark."

Mark slowly looked back at Cooper. "Son, I'm not sure yet. That's one of the reasons I have to wait to tell you. I promise you will be the only one that gets the story."

Mark sighed. "But it's not just that. To be honest, I don't want to take away attention from Gabby right now. And, quite frankly I don't want any law enforcement or state-level resources being pulled from her search. In the meantime, I truly do appreciate everything you are doing to help find Gabby."

Cooper nodded. "Soojin and I will do everything we can to get her back. In fact, I have one lead on a person connected to the kidnappers, and I think he could be our key to finding out some more information."

"See, that's what I'm looking for. Okay, get out of here and pursue your lead. Don't hesitate to call me if you need any help." He smiled grimly. "I still do have a little pull around these parts."

"I'll keep that in mind." Cooper stood.

"And, Cooper, that means if you find yourself in our local jail again, make sure to call me first." Mark winked. "Now, go get Gabby."

***

Wheeler called the governor from his car as he headed back into town. He was on a two-lane highway and traffic was starting to pick up.

"Howdy, Wheeler, what do you have for me?"

"Hello, governor. I have an update for you already. I just met with Mark and from what I gathered he has been pretty direct with the media and authorities in regards to the kidnapping. Meaning, he will make or receive phone calls to media and law enforcement, and it's all been strictly related to Gabby. At least that is my initial assessment based on direct questioning of him."

"That's good, that's what I was hoping for," said Simmons.

Wheeler suddenly laid on his car horn and swerved in the opposite lane to miss a semi-truck that pulled out in front of him. He quickly swerved back into his lane to avoid the oncoming traffic.

"What was that?" asked Simmons.

Wheeler slowly relaxed his hands' clutch on the steering wheel.

"Wheeler, what the hell was that?"

"Nothing. I'm fine." Wheeler looked in his rearview mirror at the semi behind him. "Just another damn semi that pulled out in front of me."

"Okay, is there anything else?" asked Simmons.

"When I was leaving Mark's house today someone came to visit him—a married couple named Cooper and Soojin Smith. It sounded like Soojin was close friends with Gabby and wants to help in the search for her. However, that Cooper fella, he was introduced to me as a reporter for Minnesota Public Radio. It could be nothing, but in my opinion if Mark was going to tell anyone about your deal it would be a guy like Cooper."

"What makes you say that?"

Wheeler looked out his window at the oil drills that lined the highway, an endless line of earth-penetrating machines that had been especially good to his PI business. "Think about it. Mark has a natural connection to this guy, even if it's through his granddaughter's close friend. The reporter isn't in North Dakota, so there is no fear of retaliation. And Mark can control when the story goes out, which he wouldn't be able to do with the *New York Times* or one of the other national media outlets."

Simmons clucked his tongue loud enough for Wheeler to hear it. Wheeler knew from their previous meetings that Simmons clucked his tongue when he was planning his next steps. "That's a good point. I want you to run a background search on this Cooper Smith cat and tell me everything you can about him. I may have you switch to following the reporter if he is the key to this whole thing."

Wheeler shrugged as he sped past another truck. "I'll have the information over to you by the end of the day."

***

Cooper dropped Soojin off in town so she could hang new missing person flyers for Gabby, while Cooper checked in with Fletcher about updates on the case. He used the opportunity to sneak his first smoke of the day. By the time he pulled up to the Fletcher residence, he had enough nicotine in his veins to be ready to go. Fletcher was outside pouring salt on his sidewalk.

"You think we'll get more snow?" Cooper stepped out of the rental car.

"No, but it's still wet and it's suppose to freeze tonight. This sidewalk will be glare ice if I don't prep it a bit. Where did you get the new wheels?"

"It's a rental car—my wife finally made it to town."

"Guess you won't need the snowcat anymore then," said Fletcher.

"Not for right now, but it ran great. Thanks again for lending it to me."

"You bet, anytime."

Cooper slipped his hands in his pockets. "Say, any new updates on the Gabby case? Did they find anything in the RV?"

"Believe it or not, that Nash guy must have wiped the RV clean. Makes sense with his background in law enforcement—he must know all the tricks."

"Yeah, he was a Texas Ranger, so that makes sense." Cooper walked over to help Fletcher with the salt.

"Oh, thanks." Fletcher handed him a bag. "Yeah, we have a conference call with the Rangers tomorrow to see if we can get access to his files. Maybe it will tell us something. The biggest news, though, is we think there is only one kidnapper now—just Nash."

"Really?"

"There was video footage captured at the Dickinson airport that showed the kidnapper's stolen vehicle exit the parking lot. We got a clear shot into the car and there was only one person in the front seat, and we believe it was Nash. There were no other passengers. Doesn't mean Gabby wasn't with him—he could have stuck her in the trunk or on the floor, but why wouldn't Doyle be sitting shotgun, or at least in the back seat?"

"That's a good question. Did Doyle grab a different vehicle?"

"Maybe, but we checked every car that left the airport from the time Nash ditched the RV until the storm struck, and there was no one even coming close to matching his description. And why would he stick around?"

"That's a good point. I wonder what happened to him," said Cooper. "Hey, random question, but that Nickels guy, the one that I got into a scuffle with. Is he still locked up in your jail?"

"He was just released today after lunch, but I'm sure he'll be right back again. He's done that a few times, you know. Every time he gets out of jail he goes straight to the saloon downtown and drinks himself into a stupor."

"Oh yeah? Which one does he usually go to?"

Fletcher slipped a little in the steepest part of his driveway, then quickly regained his balance. "There are a few down there, but the one we usually find him causing trouble at is a bar and grill called The Roughriders Watering Hole. Don't get caught up in all that though, it's not worth it. Things get rough down there all the time."

"Thanks for the tip."

Fletcher finished emptying his bag of salt and looked at Cooper. "I hate to tell you this, but with the holidays fast approaching, we'll be facing police understaffing issues that could hinder the Gabby search. And each day that goes by means less of a chance of finding her, which means other law enforcement agencies are going to be less likely to help out. It's a resource issue."

Cooper shook his head. "I appreciate you being candid with me, but it's still a little disheartening to think about."

Fletcher turned his hands up. "I know, I know. There is only so much we can do, especially this time of year. I pray we can find her soon, but we will have obstacles to overcome."

"Point well taken," said Cooper. "Say, I'm going to go pick up my wife. You don't mind if she stays here with me tonight, do you?"

"Of course not. I'll have Linda set out some extra towels for her."

"That'd be great." Cooper emptied his bag of salt and headed back toward his rental vehicle. Right before he reached for the door, he stopped and turned back to Fletcher. "Hey, I almost forgot. You think you could sell me one of those bottles of Dakotah Beard Oil you have downstairs?"

"Oh, you saw that, huh?" Fletcher laughed, then stroked his beard. "Linda thinks I'm crazy, but I swear by that stuff. If we ever are holed up in our basement for any extended period of time, at least I'll live out my remaining days with a good-smelling and soft beard. The answer, though, is yes. I'll make sure you get a bottle before you check out."

"You're a good man, Officer Fletcher. This place needs more people like you."

He chuckled. "Well, they can't all be good, or I'd be out of a job. The more roughnecks we have around here, the more job security I have."

Cooper laughed and got into his car.

North Dakota. The Peace Garden State.

CHAPTER 11

The Louisiana Bayou

Gabby thought she was dreaming when she heard singing. She recognized the song and the voice, but she hadn't heard it for a long time. She opened her eyes and looked over toward the sound. Sitting across the room from her was Nash, who was reading the back of a cassette tape while a stereo played next to him. He noticed her movement and turned the volume down slightly.

"I'm sorry I woke you," said Nash. "I actually thought the music would help you sleep better. Please tell me you like Elvis Presley."

Gabby sat up and stretched her right leg, the one not chained to the table. "My grandfather used to listen to Elvis all the time. Which song is this again?"

"*Are You Lonesome Tonight*? It's one of my favorites. It was one of the first songs Elvis recorded in 1960 after returning from his time with the army in Germany. He recorded it in RCA's studio B in Nashville." Nash's excitement built as he talked. "Did you know that he actually recorded it in the dark?"

"No, I didn't know that." *This guy doesn't seem like the Elvis Presley fan club type to me,* thought Gabby.

"Yeah, can you believe it? He actually had them kill the lights and they did the entire song straight through in the dark."

"So you're a big Elvis fan?" asked Gabby.

"You could say that." Nash reached over and grabbed the notepad sitting next to him. "While you were sleeping I came up with a list of my top seven favorite Elvis Presley songs." Nash read them out loud to Gabby.

BEST OF ELVIS:
1. It's Now or Never
2. Are You Lonesome Tonight?
3. Suspicious Minds
4. Good Luck Charm
5. She's Not You
6. All Shook Up
7. Burning Love (Only good song during his obese years)

"Why do you write seven things down? Why not five or ten?" asked Gabby.

Nash looked a little flustered. "It has to be seven."

Gabby pressed further. "Why?"

"It's just a thing I have, okay? It's not a big deal."

"How often do you write lists like these?"

"A few times a day." Nash sheepishly put the notepad down behind him.

"How long have you been doing this?"

"Since I was a kid."

This guy has some sort of serious OCD complex.

"Where did you grow up?" asked Gabby.

"Texas, born and raised. You?"

Gabby knew the more information she had on Nash, the better chance she could possibly use it against him later. She also didn't want to give him too much about herself for the very same reason.

"North Dakota. Where in Texas? What was your childhood like?"

Nash shifted in his chair and turned the volume on the stereo down even further so it was barely audible. "We lived in Amarillo, up in the panhandle. I grew up on a cattle ranch just outside of town. It had been in my family for three generations and my father wanted to pass it down to me, but I refused and went a different direction."

"Which direction was that?" asked Gabby.

Nash exhaled and looked away. "The military. After the 9/11 terrorists attacks I knew I had to do something to fight back. I did three tours in Iraq and one in Afghanistan with the marines. When I came back my father wanted me to take over the ranch, but instead I joined the Texas Rangers. I figured I had gained all of those skills in the marines, so why not apply them to law enforcement back in my home state?"

Gabby sized up Nash, comparing him to the stereotypical image she had of what a Texas Ranger would look like. She decided he had the hard look of authority that military and law enforcement officers had by the virtue of their chosen careers. "What was it like being a Ranger?"

Nash sat up straight and puffed out his chest. "It was a dream job, really. It was the best job I've ever had. It was a celebrated position, and people really looked up to you when you wore the badge, especially in Texas. There is a long history with the Rangers, they are as old as Texas itself. I was just glad I could be apart of it for a few years."

Gabby turned her hands up in question. "Why did you leave then?"

Nash slumped back down in his chair and took a deep breath. "It's a long story. I'd rather not get into it."

"I'd like to know."

Gabby watched Nash massage the back of his neck as he looked away again.

"There were other opportunities. I heard about all the guys heading up to North Dakota making money hand over fist working the oil fields. I thought it was my chance to get rich quick."

Well, that was a lie, Gabby thought. *Something bad must have happened.*

"Seriously, though. How do you go from being a Texas Ranger to a roughneck in North Dakota? Seems like a few steps down."

Even in the dimly lit room, Gabby could tell Nash was getting red.

"I'd rather not talk about it. Let's talk about you."

Gabby held her ground. "No, this is important. Why did you leave the Rangers? Why did you come to North Dakota?"

Nash held up his hands defensively. "Lets just say things didn't work out with the Rangers, and leave it at that. As for North Dakota, I needed a change of scenery and the oil boom provided a chance for that. Plus, I've lived in enough terrible conditions in the marines—I knew I could take the temporary housing and cold weather up there."

"Were you ever married?" asked Gabby.

"I was engaged once, to a girl from my hometown. Things just didn't work out; I got deployed overseas and we went our separate ways. It's for the best, since I found you now."

Is he living in his own fantasy world? 'I found you now.' What is that?

"I have a hard time believing someone with your background and worldly experiences didn't have the nerve to just come up and talk to me. Or why didn't you just call or email me? I'm on the city council—my information is posted on the city website."

He spread his hands in frustration. "Again, I read and heard all those bad things you said about us roughnecks and I knew you wouldn't talk to me. I had to get you in an environment so we could talk, just like we are doing now."

"How about this: I'll promise to talk to you about anything, anytime, if you let me go. I'll give you all of my phone numbers and email addresses. We can stay in touch for as long as you'd like."

"Where would you go?" asked Nash.

"Back to Williston, of course."

Nash's shoulders dropped. "That's what I thought. I was hoping we could start a new life together somewhere where it's warm. Maybe in Mexico or somewhere else in Latin America."

Gabby gave him a look of disbelief.

"Come on, it would be fun," said Nash. "We could live in an exotic place and really get to know each other. We'd both be so far removed from the frozen tundra of North Dakota, and away from all the oil problems."

"What about all of our family and friends? You just expect both of us to leave and never talk to them again?"

He shrugged. "There are ways to communicate with them securely, once we are established somewhere remote. As for me, my parents died this year and I don't talk to my brother anymore. I won't be missed."

Gabby wanted to go off on this guy. She wanted to describe to him in detail how bizarre his fantasy really was. That she hadn't even known him before he kidnapped her, drugged her, killed a guy, and brought her to the swamp in the middle of nowhere. Yes, Gabby wanted to lay into this guy good. But she didn't. She decided to play his game to see where it would lead.

"I don't think we can properly get to know each other here in this swamp. In fact, I don't even know what day it is down here, and I can't think straight with the humidity and mosquitos buzzing around outside. I hate mosquito-infested areas. When are we leaving?"

Nash's eyes lit up. "Well, we've been here for almost a week, and I plan to stay for one more week while things settle down. Usually after ten days of looking, search crews give up and go back to business as usual. That is when we can make our break."

"One more week, huh?" Gabby looked over at the stove and saw Nash had made pasta. "Want to pass me a plate of that spaghetti?"

Nash smiled and quickly jumped up to grab her a plate of food.

Seven days of acting, thought Gabby. *Then I make my great escape.*

CHAPTER 12

Williston, North Dakota

Cooper knew he should steer clear of a heavily lubricated Nickels at a bar in downtown Williston on a Friday night, but it had been almost a week since Gabby disappeared, and he needed answers. He wore a light disguise consisting of a baseball hat and a pair of old reading glasses that he found buried in his travel bag. He also decided to cut his beard into a mustache, partly to change his look but also to mirror Nickels. The beard trim was a tough decision, especially given the recent discovery of Fletcher's beard oil, but he had to take every edge he could get.

Soojin dropped Cooper off a few blocks from the bar, and he walked down the dimly lit street. As soon as Soojin was out of sight, Cooper lit up an American Spirit and fought the cold and wind as he raced to finish the cigarette before he arrived.

He was now directly across the street from the bar, and he could see *The Roughriders Watering Hole* spelled out in cursive letters illuminated by bright neon-colored lights. Beside the name was an illuminated logo of a bucking bronco with a cowboy on its back. Cooper could see through the windows that the place was packed. About a dozen people stood outside smoking cigarettes and talking.

Here goes nothing.

Cooper stopped in the doorway to take in the scene. Country music blared overhead, and men in flannel shirts and baseball hats packed the bar. As they clinked glasses together, Cooper noticed most of the tables had two or three pitchers of beer on them. The whole place smelled like a great big beer bubble bath. The high-top tables were up front, occupied by groups of five to ten men standing around each of them. More men nestled up against a traditional long bar as they drank and ordered rounds. Four enormous flat-screen televisions playing a college hockey game hung over the bar—the Fighting Sioux of North Dakota against the Minnesota Gophers, airing live from the Ralph Englestad arena in Grand Forks.

Cooper spotted Nickels at the bar, his flavor-saver of a mustache soaked through with beer. Cooper inched behind him toward another television that was playing the news and slid into an open chair in the back. A couple of waitresses were busy running around taking orders. One spotted him and asked what he was drinking as she walked past. She was young, maybe in her early to mid-twenties, and she was in a hurry. Cooper would not be her top buyer for the night, and she knew it.

"One tall Summit on tap, please." Cooper was impressed they carried the Saint Paul-based beer here in Williston.

The waitress just nodded and dashed away into the crowd. Cooper looked over at the front door, then at Nickels, and then at his phone. He sent a text message.

Center of the bar with a green hat on and ridiculous mustache.

Then Cooper looked up at the television, which announced a breaking news alert. He couldn't hear it, but scrolling subtitles reported a flash fire at a drill in Watford City late the night before. A kid from Fargo was killed instantly, and another man was airlifted to Regions Hospital in Saint Paul. When they showed the picture of the second man, Cooper recognized him right away.

Marshall.

He had suffered severe third-degree burns and was in critical condition.

Not Marshall, that guy was a cool dude.

Cooper thought about sharing the Natty Ice beer with Marshall in his RV as they talked football and Texas. He made a note to stop by and see him when he was back in Saint Paul. His phone dinged with a new message.

Is his mustache as ludicrous as yours? :) Be right in.

Cooper smiled and looked back up in time to see Soojin walk through the front door. She took off her coat and revealed her outfit.

She was dressed to kill.

She wore skintight black leather pants with knee-high black leather boots. Her bright red blouse was low-cut, and her hair was piled high. Cooper watched as the men from the other tables looked over at her. Some even whispered and pointed. The fact that she was a good-looking Korean-American didn't stir much discussion in Saint Paul, but in Williston, she was an exotic spectacle.

Soojin walked directly to the bar with all eyes trained on her. She leaned up against the bar rail right next to Nickels. Cooper watched the bartender head her way and then Nickels said something to him.

Of course he would buy her a drink.

Soojin said something in response to Nickels and they shook hands.

Come on, Soojin. It's all you now.

It was a simple plan that they had rehearsed that afternoon. Cooper would go into the bar first and try to spot Nickels. Then he would sit somewhere out of the way. Soojin would then come in and hit on Nickels. She would try to get him to join her at a table and then she would elicit information about Nash, Doyle, and anything he knew about

Gabby. Cooper would be there the whole time in case anything came up.

Just like clockwork, Soojin pulled Nickels by the arm and the two of them started to move. But the only private tables were located directly behind Cooper. Before Nickels had turned all the way from his bar stool, Cooper quickly slid around the other side of the table so his back was to the room. Luckily, high-top booths stood on the other side of his table, so Cooper pretended to play on his phone as Soojin took Nickels by the arm past him. They slid into the first booth directly in front of Cooper. Even though it was just a couple feet away, Cooper couldn't see either of them over the high booths. He couldn't hear them either, so he slid back to the other side of the table so his back was right against the booth. He couldn't make out what Soojin was saying, but Nickels was belligerent enough he could hear everything coming out of his mouth.

"What did you say your name was again?" Nickels slurred.

A brief pause for the response. "I've never met anyone named So-gin before," said Nickels. "What's that? Not So-gin, but Sue-gin? What is that, like Chinese or Japanese or something?"

The waitress handed Cooper his beer and he took a big swig of it.

"What brings you to Williston?" Nickels asked, followed by another pause. "Well, if you're looking for some fun, I think you found the right place."

It killed Cooper that he couldn't hear Soojin's side of the conversation. It sounded like it was going pretty well, though. Soojin must have asked the question they rehearsed earlier: *I want to have a lot of fun, but I'm nervous after hearing a news story about a girl that was kidnapped from around here last weekend.*

"Well, I wouldn't worry about that. I knew the guys involved with that, and trust me, the one in charge will not harm a hair on that girl's head."

The one in charge will not harm a hair on that girl's head. What does that mean? Cooper had a new note up on his iPhone and was transcribing Nickels' words.

"I'll tell you why," said Nickels. "Nash was obsessed with that girl. He had some master plan about marrying her or something idiotic like that. He wouldn't talk about it much, but I got him to share some details one night when we were drinking right here at this very bar."

Cooper's mind was racing. *If Nash didn't kidnap her to kill her, but instead to try to stay with her, what happened to Doyle?*

"Doyle, I knew Doyle," said Nickels. "The man was all foam and no beer. You know what I'm saying? He couldn't pour piss out of a boot with instructions on the heel."

Real classy, Nickels. Great language to use around a sophisticated woman you're trying to pick up.

"Yeah, well my guess is Doyle went back down to some bayou in Louisiana to lay low," said Nickels. "The dude practically lived out of a houseboat down there in the swamp near Houma. As for Nash and the girl? I'm sure they are in his hometown of Amarillo, or somewhere else in Texas playing house. Knowing Nash, the whore is probably begging him for sex by now."

That's not going to sit well with Soojin.

"You have to be rough with women, that's what they really want," said Nickels.

Cooper tensed up. He had to check on her, even if he risked blowing his cover. He peered over the booth and saw Nickels make a reach for Soojin's breast across the table. Soojin blocked Nickels' hand and kicked him hard under the table. Soojin stood up from the booth and started to walk away. Nickels fell out of the booth sideways clutching his groin. He made a desperate lunge toward her with his fist and said, "You little—"

Without looking back, she planted her front foot and drove her back leg straight toward Nickels. The back kick hit him square in his mouth. The force of her boot caused his front teeth to fall out, hitting the ground less than a second before his face and body landed.

"That was badass," said Cooper. "Now, let's get out of here."

The two of them walked briskly toward the front of the bar. By now the group that was with Nickels saw the commotion. Three men came over and met Cooper and Soojin in the middle of the bar. The big one in the middle looked like a brawler, with a smashed-in nose and strike marks on his cheeks. The one on the left was tall and scrappy-looking, while the one on the right was a short, stocky man.

Without breaking stride, the massive brawler in the center of the group came up and tried to throw a hook at Soojin's head. She ducked his punch and raised her right knee, quickly executing a perfect front kick into the man's groin. He collapsed immediately to the floor, grasping his genitals.

The scrappy man on the left moved to take a swing at Soojin. Cooper sprinted at him and speared him with the best football tackle he had in him. They ran into a bar stool, and the man lost his breath as they collapsed into a heap on the floor.

Cooper got back up and turned just in time to see Soojin strike the short, stocky man with a powerful sidekick to his neck as he charged her. He fell on top of the brawler gasping for air as he held his neck. Cooper dashed over to Soojin, briefly noting the looks of astonishment on the faces of the other patrons. Some even started to cheer.

The two of them sprinted out of the bar's front door into the cold December night. They ran all the way to the car, never looking back until they reached Fletcher's driveway ten minutes later. Cooper put the car into park and looked over at Soojin. They were both out of breath, their adrenaline high. Cooper leaned over and gave Soojin a kiss.

"That was the sexiest thing I've ever seen you do." Cooper grinned.

Soojin scowled, licking her lips.

"What is it?"

"Did you smoke tonight?"

I forgot to eat my licorice to cover up the taste of the American Spirits.

"Just a quick one," Cooper admitted. "I wanted to look casual as I was walking up to the bar."

"Casual, huh?"

Cooper looked away in embarrassment. "Yeah, you know . . . I wanted to blend in so people wouldn't notice me."

Soojin eyed him suspiciously. "If you really want to blend in, next time just shave your hideous mustache and you'll never have to worry about smoking again."

CHAPTER 13

Saint Paul, Minnesota

Cooper begrudgingly left Wellstone at an auto garage in Williston for repairs while he and Soojin took a flight back to Saint Paul. Soojin had some important meetings with the governor this week so Cooper volunteered to head south to see what he could find out about Nash and Gabby. Cooper also made a point to shave his mustache off and start fresh on what he hoped would eventually turn into a decent beard so he could use his new beard oil.

Soojin dropped Cooper off in front of MPR headquarters in downtown Saint Paul the morning after their return. Cooper stopped across the street from work for his daily ritual of reading the top headlines on the LED-lit scrolling ticker that ran across the length of the headquarters.

> *Wednesday, December 10, 2014 – Millennials Developing a Reputation as Workplace Divas...*

Sounds like something Bill Anderson would have the banner engineer put up just to make a personal point, Cooper thought. Bill couldn't stand millennials, even though they made up most of his staff. Cooper headed through the lobby and up the stairs to the third floor.

The newsroom was a massive cubicle farm. The desks had low wall partitions so you could see and yell across the room to your fellow reporter or producer. People used to call it the gopher pit, because reporters would occasionally pop their heads up and call out a breaking news story. With Wild Bill around, it was a little more like whack-a-mole, since he could smash your head in at any second with his verbal attacks.

Cooper worked in the general assignment reporting section, but had aspirations to work with the secretive and selective investigative reporting team. They sat in a different section on the other side of the third floor. The team was comprised of one senior editor and four investigative reporters, and rumor had it they were looking to expand the team.

Need to get on that team soon, thought Cooper. *Better stories and no more reporting to Wild Bill.*

Cooper got to his desk and threw his messenger bag on his chair. There was a post-it note on his screen.

Come to my office before you do anything else, but leave your hair gel. -Bill

Real funny, Bill.

Cooper marched over to Bill's office, but the door was closed. Cooper gently knocked.

"Come in," said Bill.

Cooper opened the door and Bill waved him in.

"Shut the door behind you," said Bill.

Sitting in front of Bill's desk was Lisa Larson, Cooper's adversary on the general assignments team. Lisa was the one person who stood in Cooper's way of getting the next investigative team position. She was a solid reporter, and she wanted the job as much as he did.

Cooper viewed his interactions with Lisa similar to how Jerry Seinfeld and his antagonist, Newman the mailman, used to interact on the television show *Seinfeld*—it was comprised of a mutually shared wariness and constant sizing up of each other.

Lisa turned and grinned at Cooper. She wore her signature fiery red glasses. Those things could be used by a matador in a bullfight instead of the traditional red cape. Lisa was the same age as Cooper, and tall and thin with long brown hair. Bill treated Lisa the same as Cooper because of the millennial "diva" stereotype he subscribed to.

"Hello, Lisa." Cooper eyed her suspiciously before looking over at his boss. "Bill, you wanted to see me right away? I can come back if you guys are in the middle of something."

"This concerns you both," said Bill. "Take a seat."

This can't be good.

Cooper sat down next to Lisa, who didn't acknowledge his greeting. Instead, Cooper turned his attention to Bill. Still on the good side of fifty, Bill's lack of movement over decades combined with a bald head and chubby frame made him look about ten years older than he was. He wore his standard tight sweater vest, always and forever showcasing his potbelly.

"Cooper, I'm adding Lisa as a second reporter on the North Dakota story."

"Woah," said Cooper. "I know some things have come up this past week, but don't you think it's premature to—"

Bill silenced Cooper with a wave of his hand. "No, this story is too big for even two reporters, let alone one who has a personal interest in it. I mean, I appreciate you checking in with me on a near daily basis, I really do. Your email updates helped me realize you have a couple major stories developing here. There is the oil-boom-turned-bust story with all the repercussions tied to that, and then there is the story of the kidnapping of the senator's daughter. Lisa is going to help with the first story, and you can concentrate on the kidnapping story. In fact, I'm sending Lisa to interview some of the victims and families of the workers hit by the flash fire the other night in Watford City."

Cooper tried to hold his tongue, but he couldn't. "Bill, I met the lead driller, Marshall, before he was injured. I sat and talked with him in his RV. I planned to go visit him up at Regions Hospital later today."

"There's no point," said Lisa. "I already placed a call to his nurse and she said they aren't allowing any visitors yet, not even family."

Cooper glared at Lisa then looked back at Bill.

Bill stared back at Cooper. "Here's the thing, buddy boy. You have a story right in front of you, perhaps a big-time story if you pursue it correctly. The granddaughter of a prominent politician in North Dakota was kidnapped by a couple of redneck roughnecks in his backyard. I want your full attention on that story. Lisa, on the other hand, will work the flash fire and go see what she can find out about these reports coming in about a spillage."

"Come on, Bill—"

"Regarding the spill," Lisa cut Cooper off. "I placed some calls and it sounds like it could be one of the biggest spills yet in the Bakken oil reserve. Some local experts are saying that up to three million gallons of fracking wastewater has spilled from a leaking pipe in western North Dakota near Williston. This waste has been known to destroy ecosystems by poisoning plants and killing off vegetation."

"This is exactly why I want you to get out there and get some answers on this new developing story." Bill looked at Lisa then back to Cooper. "As for you, what is your plan?"

"Bill, can I speak to you in private?" Cooper asked. "It's important."

"For crying out loud." Bill shook his head. "Okay, Lisa, give us the room. In the meantime, start getting ready for your trip out to Williston."

Lisa nodded and left the room.

"This better be good," said Bill.

Cooper looked back and made sure the door was closed, and then turned back toward Bill. "It could be. I talked to Senator Hanson, and he said if I helped to get Gabby back then he would give me a story that could be one of the biggest of the year."

"He's just using that as leverage so you'll help get his granddaughter back. I've seen that trick used before back in my days with the *Star Tribune*," said Bill.

"I think he is sincere; he sounded pretty confident about the story he wanted to tell me. He said it had to do with a corruption and blackmail scandal in North Dakota. It could be good."

"Well, don't bank on it, sonny. Just pursue the Gabby story, and if you get anything extra from the senator it will be gravy."

"Okay, I'll do that." Cooper eyed Bill. "Are you sure about assigning Lisa to the Bakken oil field story? Can't I just work on that one after I finish the Gabby story?"

"It's your lucky day, punk. I recently started going to church with my ex-wife, and it's for this reason alone I won't chew you out of my office. But don't you ever second guess a decision I make, you hear me?"

Cooper grinned. "You're going to church with your ex-wife?"

"Wipe that grin off your face, and get out of my office. You wouldn't understand, you little twerp. You and your high-maintenance millennial friends can go talk about how you should have a thirty-hour workweek, and free lunch and all that crap. You know where you can get that?"

"Where?" asked Cooper.

"France. You can move to France tomorrow and live out the rest of your days complaining about how you don't have a twenty hour workweek while eating your baguette at a local café in Paris."

Cooper rolled his eyes. "Okay, Bill, I get it."

"All right, I've had enough of you for one day. Go get me that story or else book your one-way ticket to France and never come back to this building." Bill pointed toward the door.

"I'm on it, don't worry about me." Cooper stood up to walk out, but before he reached the door Bill had one more thing to say.

"Oh, and Cooper. Don't forget there is only one position available on the investigative team. It's either going to be you or Lisa, so guess how important this story is for the both of you."

"It's life-or-death important for Gabby, and it's potentially Peabody Awards important for MPR."

"You better hurry then, time is a ticking." Bill tapped the top of his watch.

"If you need me, I'll be in Texas."

CHAPTER 14

Amarillo, Texas

Cooper was bummed the whole flight down to Texas about having another reporter on his story, especially Lisa Larson. Since starting at MPR together, Larson had one feather in her hat from her time helping the investigative team on a trial basis with the Catholic Church scandal in Minnesota. Cooper matched and maybe even surpassed her achievement with his *Brown Sugar in Minnesota* story. Now, they were both competing on the same story. Except the story was *about* North Dakota, and Cooper was in Texas. His only hope at this point was to find Gabby, for more reasons than one. If he did, not only would he help save her, but he would also get the story from Senator Hanson. That was his only shot at getting the investigative team over Larson.

This was Cooper's first trip to Texas, but he wasn't exactly excited about visiting Amarillo. Of all the places to see in Texas, Amarillo wouldn't even make his top one hundred places to visit. But, he was there for Gabby, and he was there for work.

At least its seventy degrees warmer than Minnesota right now.

The Amarillo airport had a small-town feel to it. It was named after astronaut Rick Husband, who died when the *Colombia* spacecraft disintegrated during reentry back in 2003. A prominent bronze statue in the lobby of the airport memorialized him. Cooper walked past the statue and acknowledged the fallen hero with a tip of his Minnesota Twins baseball hat.

An American Spirit hung out of the corner of Cooper's mouth as he drove his rental car into town. He was struck by how much of an interstate town Amarillo really was. Interstate 40 cut straight through the city, and Cooper drove it from east to west watching fast food chain restaurants and brand name hotels pass him by. One unique place was on the north side of the interstate, a place called the Big Texan. It advertised a free, seventy-two-ounce steak in huge letters on the side of a bull statue. The only catch was, you had to eat the steak and all the fixings within one hour or you had to pay for the meal.

Everything has to be bigger in Texas, thought Cooper.

Cooper was staying on the west end of town, and the hotel he booked advertised being the closest to the Cadillac Ranch. A quick search online revealed that the Cadillac Ranch simply consisted of ten old Cadillac cars buried nose-end into the ground. They were spray painted an assortment of colors and were located a couple hundred yards from the interstate.

Cooper knew he wasn't here for tourism, and he was happy for that. He went straight to his hotel and checked into his room. His plan was simple: he'd get a local telephone book and call every Nash in there. Then he'd try to line up interviews with the ones who were related to the kidnapper and see what he could find out. But when Cooper opened the phonebook, he found over one hundred entries for people with the last name Nash.

This is going to take awhile.

Cooper grabbed a clean ashtray, opened a new bag of licorice, and started brewing a fresh cup of coffee. He was in it for the long haul. He grabbed the phonebook and a pen and began calling.

"Hello?" said a man with a wary voice.

"Hi, my name is Cooper Smith and I'm calling . . ." Cooper let his voice trail off once he heard the other end of the phone hang up.

Oh-for-one, nice start.

After three cigarettes had burned to ash, and thirty names had been called with no luck, the thirty-first number he dialed was answered by a woman with a heavy Southern drawl.

"Hello, who is this?"

"Hi, my name is Cooper Smith and I'm calling in regards to a missing person case."

"What do you want from me?" The woman sounded amused.

"Are you Patricia Nash?"

"Yes."

"Are you by any chance related to a Declan Nash?"

"Hmm . . ."

Cooper could tell the woman was searching her long-term memory.

"Well, I had a cousin who was named Declan, but I haven't seen or talked to him in at least five or six years. Why, is he missing?"

Cooper began scribbling notes. "No, he's not exactly missing himself, but he may have information about another missing person. Say, if you don't mind me asking, what are Declan's parents' names?"

"Oh, you didn't hear the news?" she asked in a surprised voice.

"No, what happened?"

"They were killed not too long ago. It was a tragedy, too. There was a terrible tornado that came through the county and went right over their ranch. They were so stubborn they didn't want to leave so they stayed in their home. The only problem was their home got lifted up by the tornado and whipped all the way over to the next county, them along with it. Such a shame, they were nice people."

"I'm sorry to hear about that. Did Declan have any siblings?"

"Yes, he has a brother but I can't for the life of me remember his name. He is much younger, maybe in his early twenties. I haven't seen him for ages, though, and even then he was so much younger I didn't really talk to him."

"Do you know where he lives or works?"

"Oh, right here in Amarillo, of course. All of the Nash clan lives here. I'm sure you could find him in the phonebook."

Cooper rolled his eyes. *Yeah, only seventy more names to go.*

"Thanks, do you know where he might work?"

"I've heard he works at one of the barbeque places, but I've been on a diet for as long as I've known that kid so I couldn't tell you which one. I do know it's one of the best, though."

Cooper jotted his next project on his notepad. *Find the best bbq in Amarillo.*

"Thanks, Patricia. I don't mean to take up too much of your time, just one last question. Do you know of any other Nash relatives who may know Declan a little bit better?"

"Not that I know of. Their family kind of kept to themselves, especially the last five years or so. Not sure what happened, but if you find the brother I'm sure he can tell you all about it."

"Well, I appreciate your time and information."

"My pleasure."

***

Cooper spent the rest of his first night in Amarillo doing research on the best barbeque restaurants in the city. According to TripAdvisor and Yelp, the top barbeque restaurants in Amarillo were Tyler's, Spicy Mike's, and Rudy's.

The following morning, Cooper started his search for Nash's brother at Rudy's restaurant since it was the only one open for breakfast.

Who eats baby back ribs for breakfast?

To Cooper's chagrin, when he pulled up to the red-paneled building with the bright yellow signs, an advertisement in the window said that Rudy's was serving breakfast tacos until 10 am. Cooper's cholesterol went up just walking into the place—the intense smell of cooked beef and pork assaulted him. The restaurant looked like a cafeteria set up in a barn. Red and white-checkered plastic sheets covered the tables.

Easier for cleaning. Just hose them off.

Neon signs promoted name-brand beers, and a large Texas flag hung from the ceiling. The place was empty, except for a couple of workers. Cooper went up to the counter to place his order.

"Good morning. Can I have one breakfast taco, please?"

The young woman behind the counter had a big black trucker hat on and a Rudy's T-shirt. She was clearly still half asleep.

"Sure, anything else?" She yawned.

"Yeah, I have a quick question. Do you know if a guy works here with the last name Nash?"

"Nash? Hmm . . . don't know anybody named Nash."

She looked back to the kitchen. "Hey, Frank, you know anybody named Nash that works here?"

"Nope," came the reply.

"Okay, thank you," said Cooper. "I was just curious." Cooper handed cash to her for the food.

"Take a seat, and we'll bring that taco right out for you."

Strike one.

***

Cooper watched the tumbleweeds that occasionally rolled across the streets of Amarillo as he drove, his breakfast taco from Rudy's settling in his stomach. The taco had been stuffed with all sorts of grease and goodness, and Cooper knew he would pay for it later. The other two barbeque places didn't open until 11, so Cooper killed some time driving around Amarillo. He made two stops—one at the American Quarter Horse Heritage Center and Museum, and the other at the Jack Sisemore Traveland RV Museum.

After that, Cooper had basically exhausted Amarillo's tourist attractions, so he made his way over to Spicy Mike's BarBQ Haven. It was a tiny, quaint building off the highway with red-paneled walls, a white rooftop, and a brick bottom. Just the sort of no-frills place that would serve delicious barbeque.

Cooper was clearly the first customer of the day, as a man came and opened the front door when he arrived. He didn't relish the thought of eating barbeque after his large breakfast, but he didn't want to be rude. When he got out of his car, he noticed a gas station across the street called the Toot'n Totum. A black Dodge Charger sedan was parked near the front door, with the easily recognizable red taillights that stretched all the way across the back of the vehicle. Cooper swore he had seen it once already today—perhaps at one of the museums?

Is it natural for reporters to get paranoid? Cooper *had* been followed by dangerous drug dealers as he pursued the *Brown Sugar in Minnesota* story. Several of those encounters lead to car chases and shootouts that nearly killed him. *Maybe a little paranoia is okay...*

Cooper decided to wait by his car and have a smoke to see if he could spot the driver. That was one good thing about smoking—a person could kill five-to-seven minutes standing around doing nothing other than smoking and no one would question it. By the time he finished his cigarette, no one had come out to claim the Charger. Cooper shrugged it off and headed into Spicy Mike's.

The barbeque smell hit him immediately, and his stomach instantly created extra room. Big rolls of paper towels sat prominently in the center of a few small tables, ready to clean up any hungry patrons. Three steps into the joint and Cooper's mouth started to salivate.

Gotta hand it to the South, you can't get barbeque like this up in Minnesota or North Dakota.

Cooper went up to the counter, and a middle-aged man sporting a goatee and a baseball hat came out from the back.

"You're my first customer of the day." The man's hands were full of barbeque sauce. He washed them in a sink behind the counter as he looked over at Cooper. "What can I get for you?"

"Just trying to beat the rush," said Cooper. "I'll take a plate of your most popular meal."

The man wiped his hands on a towel and gave Cooper a big smile. "That would be the beef brisket, with mac-n-cheese, mashed potatoes, and toast."

"Sounds perfect to me. Say, you wouldn't happen to be the owner would you?" asked Cooper.

"Sure am, the name's Mike." He shook Cooper's hand.

"Nice to meet you, Mike. I'm Cooper."

Mike turned his ear toward Cooper as he rubbed his goatee with his hand. "I'm picking up an accent from you. Do you live in Amarillo or just passing through?"

Cooper grinned. "That's probably my Minnesota accent you're picking up on, don't cha know?" Cooper laid the accent on thick.

Both men laughed. Mike had a deep belly laugh that shook the floorboards.

"Yeah, I'm staying in Amarillo for a little bit to check some things out," Cooper said. "I actually have a question for you. I'm looking for a guy with the last name Nash. Does anyone with that name work for you?"

Mike shook his head. "I wish I *had* more workers, but I'm pulling down most of the shifts here while I try to build the regulars up. Sorry about that."

"Not a problem at all, just curious."

"Let me go get you your brisket, I'll be right back."

"Thanks, Spicy Mike." Cooper swung his right arm and snapped his fingers in disgust.

Strike two.

***

Spicy Mike's beef brisket was to die for, but it was tough to finish the plate with all the fixings, especially after such a big breakfast. Cooper decided to head straight to Tyler's Barbeque, and use whatever willpower he had left to refrain from ordering an additional meal.

Cooper pulled off the road when he saw the big star logo that read *Tyler's Barbeque, Support Texas Barbeque.* Tyler's occupied yet another red building with a big sign in the front window that said it was open for business. By now it was Amarillo's lunch hour, and Cooper walked into a wall of noise when he entered the restaurant. Again, he noticed the signature cafeteria tables and plastic tablecloths. A queue had formed to the left in line with an illuminated sign that said *Order Here.* Cooper eyed the plates of the patrons chomping away. The food looked delicious, especially the corn bread muffins and the dessert.

Cooper finally made it to the ordering window.

"What's your most popular dessert?" he asked.

The girl behind the table slid a baking pan in front of him. "The peach cobbler is amazing here. Freshly baked."

"I'll take a slice of that."

She pointed. "Head down the line and pay there."

At the end of the line, Cooper paid a girl with pigtails and dimples for his cobbler. She looked friendly, so he asked her about Nash.

"Say, quick question. Do you happen to know anyone that works here that has the last name Nash?"

She spoke with a Southern drawl. "You lookin' for Jasper?"

"Is Jasper's last name Nash?"

"I think so." She smiled and looked over her shoulder toward the kitchen. "I don't see him back there. He might have went out back to check on the smoker. Just head out around the building toward the smell of the barbeques, you can't miss it."

Cooper returned the smile. "Thank you very much, I'll get the cobbler to go."

Outside, the smoker was easy to track down. Despite the two huge meals sitting in his stomach, Cooper was half tempted to order some brisket on his way out. He rounded the back corner of the building, and sure enough a man stood behind a giant barbeque smoker attending to the meat.

"Sure does smell delicious," said Cooper.

The man casually turned around, seeming unsurprised by the compliment. He looked to be in his twenties, and he was wearing a baseball cap that covered his face in the noontime Texas sun. He had a sturdy build despite his large stomach—probably an occupational hazard, Cooper thought.

"It's the best in the state," the man said. "Sometimes we slow cook it for three or four days just to get it soft and tender with the perfect taste."

"That sounds pretty amazing, not going to lie." Cooper reached in his pocket for his pack of smokes as he held the peach cobbler to-go bag in his other. "Say, are you Jasper Nash by any chance?"

"Sure am." Jasper took off his cap and revealed short blonde hair and bright blue eyes. "Do I know you from somewhere?"

"My name is Cooper Smith. I'm down here from North Dakota looking into something that may have involved your brother."

Jasper's shoulders slumped. "Are you a cop or something? Look, I already spoke to the police about my brother. What else do you guys want?"

"I'm not a cop. I'm actually a reporter, but I'm not looking for a story. I know the gal your brother may be with, and I want to see if I can get some information that may help find them."

"Who do you work for?"

"Minnesota Public Radio in Saint Paul, Minnesota."

"I thought you said you were from North Dakota?" Jasper put his cap back on.

"I was on an assignment out there at the time, but I came down here just yesterday looking for more answers. Would you like a cigarette?" Cooper stretched the pack toward Jasper.

"No thanks, and I'd prefer not to speak to any reporters." Jasper started to turn back to the smoker.

"Woah, hey. Like I said, this is something I'm doing for my friend—our entire conversation can be off the record."

Jasper faced Cooper again. "How do you know the girl they said my brother kidnapped?"

"She is one of my wife's best friends, and she was a bridesmaid in our wedding this year. I'm not accusing your brother of anything; I just want to help find our friend. Her name is Gabby."

Jasper sighed. "Well, what do you want to know?"

"Would it be better to meet up later after work?"

"Nah, I'm busy later. Look, if you can talk while I'm working on the meat that's fine with me."

"Works for me," said Cooper.

Jasper returned his attention to the smoker. "Okay, ask away."

Just then, Cooper noticed a car speeding away from an alley that stood between the barbecue joint and a motel. He only caught the back edge of it as it disappeared behind the motel, but it was unmistakably the bright red taillights of a black Dodge Charger.

How many black Dodge Chargers are there in Amarillo?

"Do you have any questions, or what?" asked Jasper.

Cooper turned back to Jasper. "Yes, sorry about that. So, when was the last time you talked to your brother?" He took one last look over his shoulder, but the Charger was gone.

"About three months ago. Ever since he went up to North Dakota, we only talked three or four times a year."

"Did he happen to tell you he was dating anyone or anything like that?"

"No, our parents had just died and we were making funeral arrangements."

Cooper winced. "I'm really sorry to hear about your loss."

"Yeah, well my parents are probably rolling in their graves. They wanted Declan to take over the family ranch, but he turned them down. Then they looked to me, but to be honest I have the place up for sale. Hoping to start my own barbeque joint with the proceeds. But anyway, to answer your earlier question about Declan and dating, no he wouldn't get into things like that with me. He is a really introverted guy. I bet he hasn't dated anyone since he left Texas for the Dakotas."

Cooper nodded. "That's good to know. Say, when did he leave Texas?"

Jasper looked up and closed one eye, his lips moving as he whispered to himself. "I'm trying to think of the exact year, but it's escaping me right now. It was a few years back though. He got canned by the Rangers and then he headed up north."

Cooper waved a hand. "It's fine if you can't remember the exact date. I'm curious, and if you don't mind me asking, why did the Rangers let him go?"

Jasper shrugged. "You know, we all asked him that a million times, but he would never say. He would get really mad about it, and then he would storm out of the room. My father finally confronted him one day about it and he marched right out of the house and went straight up to North Dakota without so much as a goodbye."

Cooper shook his head as he crossed his arms. "Wow, no kidding."

After several moments without a response, Cooper stepped a little closer to Jasper. "Well, did you know any of his colleagues at the Rangers who might be able to share some details?"

Jasper nodded slowly, and then paused before responding. "Yeah, I knew this one guy. He was Declan's partner. I thought about trying to look him up a few times, but figured there was no point."

"Do you remember his name?"

Jasper turned his attention back to the smoker to check the meat again. He moved a rack of ribs around and checked on another. "He goes by 'Lefty,' but his real name is Clayton Greene."

"Why Lefty?" Cooper shifted to the side of the smoker so he could get a better look at Jasper's face.

Jasper noticed the movement and turned toward Cooper. "Well, he's right-hand dominant in everything he does, except for shooting. He shoots with his left eye and hand, and he's pretty good at it from what Declan told me."

"So." Cooper paused. "Do you know where Lefty currently works?"

Jasper slowly shrugged. "I'm not positive, but I know he was working at the main Rangers' office down in Austin. That's your best bet."

Cooper nodded. "Thanks for the tip. Is there anything else you can tell me about your brother that might help find him or Gabby?"

Jasper closed the door on the smoker and pointed a finger at Cooper. "Just be careful. Between his military training, Rangers experience, and his compulsive behavior, you never know what Declan you are going to find."

Cooper's eyes grew wide. "What do you mean by compulsive behavior?"

Jasper put his foot up on the side of the trailer that the smoker sat on, and Cooper noticed his red cowboy boots. Resting his arms on his bent knee, he leaned toward Cooper. "Listen, I don't really want to get into it, but just know Declan has some weird kind of OCD where he gets fixated on things. He's had it his whole life. A casual outside observer might not notice it, but he has a problem. Every time my parents tried to get him help or medicine he would shutter away."

"How did he cope with it?" Cooper mirrored Jasper by putting his Red Wing boot on the trailer.

"I don't think he ever really did, but that's why the military and Rangers were good for him. They provided structure to his life, and he liked that. I'm not sure what happened once he got up to North Dakota. I don't think that was the best place for him to go, but I think he just wanted to get away from it all."

Cooper nodded. "That's really good to know, thanks for sharing."

Jasper eyed the back door of the restaurant, pushing off of the trailer with his boot so he stood up straight. "Look, I have to get back inside. Think you have enough to go on?"

Cooper took the cue and stood up straight, too. "I think you helped point me in the right direction. Thanks so much for your time and the details about your brother. I'll let you get back to making more of that delicious barbeque. Good luck with opening your own joint, too."

"Thanks, you'll have to try it out sometime."

Cooper shifted his bag of cobbler to his left hand and used his right one to shake Jasper's hand. "Although my belt would disagree, you can count me in."

Both men laughed and went their separate ways.

Base hit. Time to go to Austin.

CHAPTER 15

Bismarck, North Dakota

The Nixon bobblehead nodded on Governor Simmons' desk as he sat in his office chair drinking a glass of whiskey.

"You know what Nixon's greatest fault was?" asked Simmons.

"No, what?" Thompson sat on the opposite side of the desk in a leather chair sipping on his own glass of whiskey.

"He got caught."

"Yeah, he got caught big time, and so could we."

"No," said Simmons. "We won't, not if I have anything to say about it."

Thompson took a big swig from his glass and set it down on the desk. "Hey, I meant to ask you. How did your meeting with Bob's sexy intern go the other night?"

Simmons set his glass down on the desk and gave Thompson a devilish, cunning smile. "Well, when you're the governor, girls will let you get away with things."

"Like what?"

"Nothing, really. We talked most of the night right over there on those couches in front of a fire." Simmons motioned across the room. "It was a nice conversation, then at the end of the night I just gave her a goodnight kiss is all."

"Like on the cheek or what?"

"No, on the lips, of course." Simmons grinned.

Thompson shot him a look of surprise. "She didn't say anything?"

"I think she was stunned, but she just let it happen and then she was gone."

"You dog, you."

"Thanks for setting it up. I might have to have her over again some time."

Thompson raised his glass. "It's good to be king."

"It sure is."

"Hey, so it sounds like that Minnesota radio reporter you were worried about started a bar fight up in Williston," said Thompson.

"Yeah, I heard. Him and his saucy Asian wife." Simmons took a swallow of whiskey.

"How did you hear about it?"

"Wheeler. He's been on the reporter since he stopped by Hanson's place last week."

"What's the reporter's name?"

"Smith."

"Smith, huh. Where is he now?"

"Wheeler followed him over to Minnesota, and then down to Texas. Smith is going down gopher holes to find Gabby and that roughneck." Simmons laughed.

"Wheeler is down in Texas?" Thompson snickered. "That's a little outside of his range, wouldn't you say?"

"Let's give him a call and see how he's doing." Simmons turned his phone on speaker mode and dialed Wheeler.

"Wheeler here."

"Hello, Magnum PI." Simmons chuckled. "I have you on speaker phone with Thompson here. How's it going down in the Lone Star State?"

"Real funny, governor. So far I've followed Smith around Amarillo, but he seems to be chasing dead ends. He might have found one of the roughneck's relatives, but not sure where that'll get him."

"Good," said Simmons. "Let him chase the wind, that just means he won't be on our case or talking to Hanson."

"Look, it's not ideal down here. I don't know the terrain, and my work is getting sloppy. I'm by myself and can't do proper surveillance without a team. I'm afraid Smith will figure me out."

"Give him some room," said Thompson. "As long as he stays down there it shouldn't be such a concern for us."

"Yeah, well easy for you guys to say," said Wheeler. "Listen, I'm in the room next to his at this hotel in Amarillo, and I overheard him telling his wife he is heading down to Austin in the morning. I'll go there to see what he is up to, but how long do you want me to follow him?"

"Just see what he does in Austin and report back to us," said Simmons. "That's what I am paying you for."

"You're still paying me for mileage from the road trip down to Texas and back to North Dakota, right?"

"Hey, it's not my fault you're afraid of flying."

"Listen, I'm working hard for you and I expect—"

"Don't worry! Just stay on Smith and you'll be paid." Simmons ended the call.

"Well, at least Smith is distracted for a little while," said Thompson. "But, what's the play if he decides to come back to North Dakota? Should we throw him in jail for the bar fight when he returns?"

Simmons tapped a pen on his desk. "No. Smith's office already sent another reporter out to fill his shoes."

Thompson scrunched his forehead. "Who is the new reporter?"

Simmons waved off Thompson. "Relax. Her name is Lisa Larson. I put one of the undercover state troopers on her. He pulled her record and she looks pretty clean. She was born in Wisconsin, but lives in Saint Paul now and works for MPR. Sounds like she is trying to spin up stories on that recent spill."

Thompson rolled his eyes. "Give me a break, those spills are a dime a dozen. I don't care how big it is."

Simmons leaned back in his chair and put his boots up on his desk. "Yeah, well, if the *New York Times* couldn't find us out with their investigative reporting, I'm not too worried about this Larson gal from Minnesota. But, if she gets too pushy I'll just run her out of the state."

Thompson relaxed his posture. Slumping back into his chair, he took a sip of whiskey. "So what's the plan for when Smith comes back? How do we keep him away from Hanson?"

Simmons took a drink from his glass and twirled the remaining whiskey around as he responded. "I don't think we can keep him from Hanson; they will naturally talk. No, for Smith I have another idea. I'm going to invite him over for a consultation with the governor." Simmons pointed his thumb back at himself. "I'll give him a warm reception and let him know we are pulling for him to find Gabby."

"With the real purpose of?"

Simmons set his glass back down and stared right at Thompson. "Lieutenant governor, have you not learned anything from me? It's like I always say, keep your friends close, your women closer . . ."

"And the media the closest," said Thompson.

Simmons nodded. "Good. Now make a call and get him on my calendar."

"Will do, boss."

"Oh, and one more thing." Simmons smiled.

"What's that?"

"Make sure to also invite his cheeky little Asian wife for the meeting."

CHAPTER 16

Austin, Texas

Cooper tried but failed to get a last-minute flight from Amarillo down to Austin. A business-class ticket was going for seventeen-hundred dollars, but Wild Bill would literally kill him if he purchased that flight with MPR funds. So, Cooper was forced to make the seven-and-a-half hour drive south to the state's capital.

They weren't kidding about this being a massive state.

Cooper fought off sleep and boredom by drinking coffee, smoking American Spirits, eating licorice, and listening to local radio. He thought about the Dodge Charger that he suspected was following him in Amarillo. He now checked his rearview mirror every few miles. There was no sign of it since the sighting at Tyler's Barbeque, but Cooper was sure it wasn't a coincidence. He finally stopped thinking about it for a moment when he saw the little green sign with the white letters that proclaimed he had reached Austin city limits.

It wasn't exactly the trip he had imagined for his inaugural visit to Austin. Each March, Austin hosted a festival and conference called South-by-Southwest (SXSW). It featured the best of music, film, technology, and culture. Every year, Cooper read reports about it, and each time he wished he were there.

Find Gabby and then you can reward yourself with a trip to SXSW, thought Cooper. *As if extra motivation is needed.*

It was late in the afternoon, but Cooper thought he would try his luck by seeking out the Texas Ranger that Jasper had mentioned, Mr. Clayton "Lefty" Greene.

Cooper exited the highway and made his way to the Texas Department of Public Safety. The DPS headquarters was spread out over a series of connected brick buildings, located in the north part of Austin. Cooper turned off of Lamar Boulevard into the DPS visitor's center parking lot.

Just as he pulled into a parking spot, his phone rang. It was a 701 area code—North Dakota. He answered.

"Hello, this is Cooper."

"Mr. Smith?" asked a woman on the other end of the line.

"Yes."

"Hi, I'm calling from the North Dakota governor's residence, and Governor Simmons would like to invite you to dinner the next time you are in Bismarck. Please, could you tell me when that will be?"

What in the world is this about? Cooper thought.

"Wow, I'd be honored. I'm away on business right now but plan to return to North Dakota this coming weekend. Would that work for the governor?"

Cooper heard the lady shuffle some papers. "Would Sunday night at 7 pm work for you?"

Cooper checked the calendar on his phone. He was planning on staying one more day in Austin, and then he would travel back to Minnesota on Thursday. Check in with the office on Friday, and then he could drive all the way out on Saturday, and be fresh for the meeting on Sunday.

"Yes, that should work. May I ask the reason for the meeting?"

"Governor Simmons said he wanted to meet and personally thank you for all the work you've done trying to find the missing woman from Williston."

"Well, that is very kind."

"Oh, and Mr. Smith. The governor has extended the invitation to your wife, as well. He said he has a gift for her to pass on to Minnesota's governor."

"I will see if it works with her schedule, and confirm."

"That would be perfect. I'll send you additional details once you both have confirmed. Have a nice day."

Cooper looked down at his phone. *Well, that was totally random.*

Cooper called Soojin.

"Hey, cowboy. How's Austin so far?"

"Hey there, ninja. It's going pretty well. Except, I keep thinking about that car that was following me yesterday."

"I'm sure it was nothing, just your paranoia setting in. Have you seen any sign of it today?"

"No, not yet. How are things going back in Minnesota?"

"Governor Knutson is giving me flexibility to make calls about Gabby during the work day, but we are busy gearing up for the next legislative session."

"Yeah, I bet. Say, speaking of Governor Knutson, I just got off the phone with the office of North Dakota's governor. He invited both of us to dinner in Bismarck this Sunday night. He asked for you to come, because he wants to give you a gift to present to Knutson."

"I'm sure it's one of those silly gag gifts, like the time Wisconsin's governor gave Knutson a Green Bay Packers jersey after they beat us." Cooper could almost see her rolling her eyes. "Kind of strange for it to happen out of the blue though, don't you think?"

"Yeah, it's a bit weird. The secretary did say he wanted to thank us for the work we've done looking for Gabby."

"Well, we haven't found her yet," said Soojin.

"Maybe he wants to offer additional resources, or maybe it was something Senator Hanson set up for us."

"That could be." She paused. "Okay, count me in. How much longer will you be down in Texas?"

"I'm about to go talk to one of Nash's old coworkers from when he was with the Texas Rangers. If he is willing to talk I could be out of here soon. Hope to be back up home late on Thursday night."

"Sounds good, keep me posted."

"Will do."

Cooper set his phone down and saw it was 4:30 pm. Maybe he could get lucky and catch Ranger Greene before he headed out for the day. Cooper grabbed one more piece of licorice for the walk and chewed on it as he got out of his car. He made his way up to the visitor center, an unassuming brick building. In the main lobby, a white man who appeared to be over three-hundred pounds was attempting to pull off a Fu Manchu-style mustache. He sat at the receptionist counter watching the clock on the wall.

Soojin would kill me if I rocked the Fu Manchu, Cooper thought.

"Excuse me," Cooper said.

The man slowly turned his gaze away from the clock. "Can I help you?"

"Yes, I'd like to see Ranger Clayton Greene, please?"

He started typing something on his computer. "Do you have an appointment?"

"Nothing official. I just needed to talk to him about an ongoing case that he may be able to shed some light on."

The man kept typing on his computer, not looking up. His fingers were too large for some of the keys, so he kept

116

deleting his accidental key strikes and re-typing. "Who are you with?"

"Minnesota Public Radio."

The man looked up for a moment like Cooper was crazy, then looked back down and started typing more. "Can you show me your identification and credentials?"

Cooper slid his driver's license and press credentials to the man.

"Just have a seat over there and I'll see if he is available." The man motioned to a small sitting area.

"Thank you so much."

So much for Southern hospitality.

Cooper sat down and found himself also staring at the clock. It was now 4:40 pm, and he knew that each minute closer to five meant less of a chance that he would get a meeting today.

At 4:50, Mr. Fu Manchu called out to Cooper. "He'll be down in five minutes. You can have your ID back now."

"Sounds good, thanks for your help." Cooper walked over and grabbed his ID.

If Chuck Norris walks through the door, I'm going to die.

A side lobby door opened, but Norris did not walk out. Instead, a confident black man stepped into the lobby looking like a poster boy for the Rangers. He wore the traditional white cowboy hat and a pristine white dress shirt with an orange tie and silver tie clip. The Ranger badge was pinned prominently over his heart, and he had on dress slacks with a pistol on his belt loop. The sound of his footsteps in his cowboy boots echoed across the lobby. He was over six feet tall with a solid build.

A real-life Texas Ranger. Hot dang.

"Mr. Smith?" he asked as Cooper walked over to meet him.

"Mr. Greene?"

"Yes, you wanted to meet me?"

Cooper held out his hand. "Nice to meet you. I was hoping to ask you just a few quick questions."

Greene looked up at the clock. "Well, visitor hours are over, but I have to walk out to my truck, so why don't you take a walk with me."

"Sounds great."

Greene motioned for Cooper to follow him to the back door, waving to Mr. Fu Manchu on his way out. "So, you're a reporter down here from Minnesota?"

"Yes, but I've been working in North Dakota on a kidnapping case that involves your old partner—I'm sure you've heard of it."

Greene directed Cooper through another set of doors, and then they were outside. "Yes, we got a call from the police department up in Williston, North Dakota about Nash. We turned over his file to them to aid in the investigation. Unless Nash turns up in Texas—" Greene stopped and looked directly at Cooper—"which he won't, we are washing our hands of him. Just as we did a few years back when he was cut from the force."

"Why don't you think he would come to Texas?"

"This is all off the record, right?"

"Sure."

Greene stopped walking. "Okay, well before I tell you anything, you need to tell me something. Why are you so interested in this kidnapping? You trying to get a big story?"

"No, sir. I actually know the woman who is missing. She was in our wedding party a few months back, and she is close to my wife."

Greene nodded and began walking again. "I suppose that is a good enough reason for your interest."

"Yes, and so far the other law enforcement agencies working on it have come up short. It's been almost two weeks since she disappeared, and the likelihood of finding her—"

"The chance of her being alive at this point is statistically small, I know." They arrived at Greene's truck, a brand new silver-colored Dodge Ram pickup. Greene ceremoniously patted it on the hood.

"Nice truck," said Cooper. "Is it brand new?"

"Sure is, they are the first Texas Ranger concept trucks. Take a look." Greene opened the driver's side door.

Cooper came around the door and peered in. The interior sported a custom brown leather interior with horse saddle designs. The center console showcased a large Texas Rangers badge sewn into the leather. Cooper took a deep breath.

"I love the smell of a new vehicle. You can't beat it, and the interior design on this is awesome."

Greene smiled. "You got that right. Okay, so I'll fill you in on a few things—but again this is all off the record and is intended only to be used to help find your friend. Got it?"

"Works for me. Want a cigarette?" Cooper showed Greene the label on his cigarettes.

Greene waved him off. "Don't you know those things will kill you?"

"That's what my wife tells me." Cooper put the pack back in his pocket without lighting one.

Greene leaned against the side of the truck and looked off into the distance. "The reason I don't think he is in Texas is because Nash knows all the law enforcement tricks. He literally knows every move authorities have made since he took the woman. One of the first things police like to do when there is a kidnapping is talk to the family and friends of the kidnapper to see if he has reached out to them in any way. Perhaps he contacted a relative asking for help, or to borrow a friend's car, but Nash knows all that. He wouldn't do it."

"Yeah, I actually got your name from his brother, Jasper, up in Amarillo. He said he hasn't heard from Declan, but that you would be a good person to talk to. He even called you Lefty and said he used to know you."

Greene's eyes lit with recognition. "Jasper, that's right. I haven't thought of him in years. Lefty is my nickname; it seems like a rite of passage around here to get a nickname. So, like I said, I'm not surprised he didn't reach out to his brother or any other family. The reason I don't think he is in Texas is he is not going to go anywhere that he has already been before."

"How come?" Cooper leaned against the truck as well.

"Police tend to look at all the places someone has been before to see if there are any possible connections that could suggest he would return there. Nash knows all that, so he won't be hiding out in any of the states he has spent time in."

"Well, you were his partner—where *has* he been?"

Greene stroked his chin. "I seem to recall he used to make road trips for work out to California. He would stop in Albuquerque, Phoenix, and eventually Los Angeles. He worked with various law enforcement elements on some of our cases, the ones that had ties outside of Texas. Also, I highly doubt he could have left the country, especially if the girl is alive. With biometrics being what they are now, he would have a difficult time getting across a border, unless he was smuggled."

"My guess is he went south or southeast from North Dakota," said Cooper. "A massive snowstorm was making its way east from Montana on down to Colorado around the time he left. There is no way he could have gone in that direction. Also, we know he went south to a different city in North Dakota to get rid of his RV and steal a vehicle."

"And you can assume he wouldn't stay in North Dakota," said Greene. "Or any of the states in the drive path from Texas on up, since he likely drove through those places on his trips to and from oil country."

Cooper thought about this. "Great . . . so, that leaves pretty much any state on or east of the Mississippi River." Cooper shook his head. "He could be anywhere."

"At least you've cut your search down by half the country. It's a start, but I think you're looking at this all wrong." Greene turned, resting his right arm on the truck bed so he was facing Cooper.

Cooper turned toward him. "How so?"

"I think you should focus on who he knew and talked to up in North Dakota. My guess is he used someone up there unwittingly to plan out this whole scenario. That's one thing you have to know about Nash. He is a meticulous planner; he thinks about ten steps down the road. He does not leave things to chance. So, wherever he went, he had things lined up in advance. Knowing Nash, he wouldn't make any specific arrangements himself—he would have used a cut out so he could avoid leaving a trace."

Cooper slumped his shoulders. *Great, so Nash knew Marshall, who is in the hospital, Nickels, who wants to kill me, and Doyle, who is God knows where.*

"That makes sense," said Cooper. "I think I'll work on that when I get back up north. Now, I have another question for you. Your career seems like one of the most prestigious law enforcement jobs out there. So why did Nash quit the Rangers?"

Greene laughed. "He didn't quit—he was fired!"

"Fired, huh. Why is that funny?"

Greene leaned in a little closer. "Okay, let me tell you one quick story, but this will have to be the end of our conversation. You see, my lady is cookin' up some good stuff tonight, and I want to make it home while it's still warm."

"No problem. What's the story?"

Greene smiled. "I can laugh about it now, but at the time it was a serious issue for our department. You see, Nash used the same tactic every time he interviewed a suspect. He would write up a list of seven things that could happen to the suspect if he or she didn't cooperate. It was always seven things, not six or eight, it had to be seven. Part of his OCD or whatever he had. Anyway, he would write it out directly across the table from the person being interviewed in one of our interrogation rooms. Most suspects would just ignore him, but this one guy—" Greene shook his head. "This one guy called Nash a crazy cowboy. If there is one thing Nash hates more than being called a cowboy, it's being called crazy. He was once engaged to a girl who jokingly called him crazy one day and he called off the wedding on the spot."

"No kidding. That's a little extreme," said Cooper.

"Yeah, so anyway, this suspect calls Nash a crazy cowboy, and before you could even bat an eye, Nash whips out a knife from his belt and stabs it straight through the man's right hand so it's stuck to the table." Greene chuckled. "The guy is screaming bloody murder, and Nash is just shouting at him saying, 'Am I crazy now? Am I crazy now?' until the guy passes out."

"Wow, that's . . . well, that's crazy." Cooper laughed.

"Of course the guy sues the department and there is this big lawsuit. Management let Nash go immediately to avoid losing their jobs, and the next thing you know he is gone. Went up to the middle of nowhere North Dakota to drill for oil."

"Dang, that's quite the story."

"Like I said, I can laugh now, and maybe that kind of cowboy stuff used to fly back in the rowdy early days of the Rangers, but not today. The suspect ended up getting off of his charges and won a lawsuit against the Department of Public Safety. It cost the department and taxpayers millions of dollars. So, you can understand why everyone here has washed their hands of him."

"I sure can. Say, I don't want to hold you from your dinner, but I do appreciate your time."

The men shook hands. "Best of luck on your search. I hope you get your friend back." Greene jumped into his truck and rolled down the window.

"Hey, how many black Dodge Chargers would you say there are in Texas?" asked Cooper.

"That's a random question—why do you want to know?"

"Just curious is all."

"I'd say they are as common as armadillos around here."

Cooper smiled. "Good to know, thanks."

"Later, partner." Greene rolled up his window and sped away.

Cooper chuckled to himself. *As common as armadillos... You don't hear that up in Minnesota very much.*

CHAPTER 17

The Louisiana Bayou

Gabby could hear Nash swearing as he worked on the houseboat's ignition. The engine wasn't firing, and Nash was getting more and more upset with each failed attempt. Nash told Gabby earlier in the morning that it had been two weeks since they left Williston, and it was now time to leave for the next location. The only problem with his plan was the houseboat wouldn't start and they were stuck in the middle of the bayou.

"I thought you knew what you were doing!" Gabby called out to Nash after another failed attempt.

He stopped and turned toward Gabby. "I do, but this piece of crap isn't starting for some reason. Once I have it fixed we will be well on our way." He turned back to try again.

"You're going to flood it if you keep doing that."

"It'll be fine, I've almost got it."

The engine started making a loud whining noise and then something sounded like it snapped. Then silence.

"No, no, no!"

"I told you." Gabby smiled. This was the first time she had seen Nash visibly upset. His master plan was failing, and this might provide her with an opportunity to get away.

Nash had finally removed Gabby's chain, so she was sitting in the houseboat's living room chair. Nash stormed past her toward the back of the houseboat, cursing along the way. Gabby heard him open a compartment that must have been where the engine was located. He exhaled loudly and started banging on something. Once he was finished he came back into the living room and looked at Gabby.

"We have a slight problem." Nash's voice was shaky.

"You think? What are we going to do now?"

"Hold on, let me check something."

Nash went to the edge of the room and pulled a ladder down from the ceiling, which led to a trapdoor that opened up to the roof of the houseboat. He climbed all the way up, and Gabby heard his footsteps above her. She thought she could hear him untying straps, but couldn't be sure. A few moments later she heard a splash outside the window of the houseboat. Then she saw two paddles come down through the trap door along with two life jackets.

Does he seriously think we are going to paddle out of here?

Nash climbed back down the ladder and picked up a paddle and life jacket, handing them to Gabby.

"Here, try this vest on and make sure it fits. There is a canoe out there we can use to get out of here. I just have to pack some supplies first."

"How far will we go?" she asked.

"Further than I'd like, so we'll have to leave soon. We won't have the cover of darkness to protect us, but we will be quiet when we get back to town."

"What town?"

"Don't worry about that, just try on that jacket."

Gabby set the paddle down and put on her life jacket, pulling it snug as she peered out the side window. She could barely see a canoe sitting next to the houseboat on top of the water, attached only by a single rope. Gabby turned and saw Nash was in the back of the boat getting supplies ready for the trip.

This may be my only chance to get away, and with it ensure Nash is stuck out here. The question is, can I find another boat or somebody else to guide me to safety?

Adrenaline rushed through her. She grabbed her paddle and snuck up to the front of the boat. She eased the door out slowly. She was on the deck area and could see the canoe sitting on the green, swampy water, connected to the middle section of the houseboat.

Gabby crept along the houseboat's deck until she reached the rope tied to the canoe. If Nash came back to the living room she would be exposed, so she stayed low. The rope had an old weathered knot attached to a hook on the side of the houseboat. The knot looked like it had been glued into place by the forces of weather. She inspected the knot closer while keeping one eye up on the window to see if Nash was coming. She tried to recall her days as a scout leader for her local Girl Scouts program.

Which knot is this one again? Is this a bowline? It has to be.

Gabby set her paddle softly down on the deck and grabbed the knot. After a few seconds that felt like an eternity, Gabby found the knot's end. She was able to push it back through the loop. She heard a cabinet shut inside the houseboat and her body froze as her heart raced. She peered up through the window to see if she could spot Nash, but he must have still been in the back room.

She pulled hard on the rope and was able to thread the rope's end through one of the loops. She was halfway to untying it when she heard Nash.

Nash shook the houseboat as his feet pounded with each step. "Hey, where did you go? Where are you?"

Gabby's heart was beating out of her chest as she untied the rest of the rope. She turned and threw her paddle in the canoe, kicking it away from the houseboat as she scrambled in.

Nash spotted her from inside and came bursting onto the deck. "Hey, wait! Where do you think you're going?" He threw a bag down that he had been carrying and kicked his boots off. "Stop right now, don't make me get in there!"

Gabby frenetically tried to situate her paddle to row, but a huge cypress tree blocked her way. She tried to push off of it with the paddle as Nash jumped into the water and started to swim at her.

Come on, come on, paddle.

Gabby was able to navigate around the tree, but right before she hit an open patch of water the canoe jerked and dipped backward. Nash had caught up with her.

"Stop right now!" he commanded.

"Let go!" Gabby paddled frantically, but Nash held on and started to rock the canoe.

"Stop now or you're going under!" he warned.

Gabby turned and tried to hit Nash over the head with the paddle. He let go of the canoe and slid around to the other side. Gabby rotated her body and took another swing on the other side, this time hitting Nash square on top of the head.

He went under for a split second, then came out of the water with both hands extended as he lunged at Gabby. She wasn't ready for the attack, and he grabbed her arm. He pulled her into the water as the canoe capsized. The water was dark and thick with algae.

Gabby's life jacket restricted her movements as she tried to fight Nash underwater. He pulled both of them up as he grabbed onto a cypress tree. Gabby choked up water she had swallowed. Nash tossed her over an exposed root of the tree as she continued to gag.

"Stay right there," he ordered.

Gabby turned to see Nash swim to the overturned canoe. He grabbed it before swimming with it back to the cypress tree. Finding the attached rope, he held onto it as he swam back to the houseboat, about fifty feet away. He tied the end of the capsized canoe to the houseboat. When he looked back at Gabby, he had terror in his eyes.

"Swim!" he yelled.

Gabby looked over her shoulder and saw a set of eyes in the open water moving directly toward her.

She tried to cry out, but her body took over and she dove into the water and started swimming frantically back toward the houseboat. The life jacket slowed her progress. Nash jumped up on the deck of the houseboat and grabbed something out of the bag he had dropped earlier. Gabby's heart skipped a beat when she saw it was a gun, pointed right at her.

"Keep swimming! If he gets close I'll take him out," Nash cried.

Gabby continued toward the houseboat. She was about ten feet away when she saw the muzzle flash and heard bullets whiz over her head.

Paralyzed with fear, she floated the rest of the distance to the houseboat holding onto her life jacket. Nash reached down and pulled her onto the deck of the houseboat. She started shaking as Nash stripped off her life jacket and held her in place.

Gabby didn't fight him; her energy was spent. About ten feet away, a massive alligator floated on top of the water, belly-up and riddled with bloody bullet holes.

So much for my big escape.

CHAPTER 18

Bismarck, North Dakota

The thermometer in central North Dakota registered at ten degrees Fahrenheit as Cooper and Soojin drove from their hotel to downtown Bismarck. The dinner with the governor was scheduled for 7 pm, and since it was only 5:30, they decided to stop by JL Beers, a local sports bar, to grab a drink. It was in an old brick building located on Third Street, just a few blocks away from where they would be having dinner.

"Brrr . . ." Cooper shivered as he stepped into the parking lot.

"Quite a shock after that Texas heat?" teased Soojin.

"Yeah, I think I could get used to that weather. This is too cold. It's only December. What's it going to be like here in January?"

"Let's get inside."

They shuffled around the building and went inside. JL Beers consisted of a long and narrow room, with low ceilings and dim lights hanging from the rafters. Only a few other patrons occupied the space. Cooper and Soojin sat down at two empty bar stools in the center of the bar. A couple television screens played ESPN above.

"What're you two drinking?" asked a bearded, college-aged bartender wearing a bright green John Deere hat.

Soojin looked down at a drink menu while Cooper looked up at the at-least forty beers on tap.

"I'll get a glass of your in-house beer, the one you call *Watering Hole*," said Cooper.

"Sure thing, and for you?" The bartender looked at Soojin.

She glanced up from the menu with a smile. "Do you really have Schell's 1919 Root Beer on tap?"

"You bet we do."

"Perfect, I'll have a glass of that."

"Coming right up." The bartender turned away to get the drinks ready.

"Nice choice," said Cooper. "Way to support a made-in-Minnesota root beer. I guess you're driving tonight."

"Well, I figure after what happened last time I was in a bar in North Dakota, I should probably lay low."

Cooper laughed and leaned back on his stool, checking out Soojin's shoes. "You're not wearing those killer boots this time. I miss those things."

Soojin laughed. "Rest assured, I could do just fine in a fight with any foot attire."

"I don't doubt you for one second."

The bartender brought the drinks over. Cooper and Soojin clinked their glasses together.

"To Gabby."

"To Gabby."

They both took long drinks.

"Mmm, this root beer never gets old," said Soojin.

"Mine is good, too."

Soojin set her glass down and looked at Cooper. "What did Fletcher say when you updated him on your trip down to Texas?"

Cooper grimaced. "He reiterated that their department and every other police department in the country is understaffed right now, so the search for Gabby is not going to get the resources it needs."

Soojin lowered her head.

Cooper continued. "He also said that any leads we discover outside of North Dakota would technically be outside of their jurisdiction. That means they can try to coordinate with those local law enforcement agencies, but there is nothing they can do to track down those leads themselves."

They both sat in silence for a few moments, taking sips of their drinks. Soojin turned so she was facing Cooper. "I'm glad you were able to talk to Nash's brother, and his old partner with the Rangers."

Cooper nodded, taking a sip of his beer. "I've been thinking about both of those meetings a lot, especially the conversation with Greene. That guy said he would bet money that Nash used someone up here to line up his escape without them knowing about it."

"That should be easy to figure out; he was only connected to a few people up here," said Soojin.

"I know, but one is Nickels, who obviously isn't going to talk to us. Another is Marshall, who is still in the intensive care unit at the hospital, and the last one is Doyle. We have no idea what happened to Doyle."

"Maybe he's the one. We could focus on him."

"Yeah, but what about the videotape at the airport?" Cooper ran his hands through his hair. "He wasn't there, it was just Nash."

"Doesn't mean Nash didn't use him to plan his escape."

"True." Cooper took a long swig of his beer. It was refreshing despite the cold weather. Cooper looked up at the television, which played highlights from the day's NFL games. The New Orleans Saints had played host to the Atlanta Falcons earlier, and the highlights included a Falcons defensive sack on Drew Brees, which lead to a fumble, recovered by Atlanta. The Saints lost fourteen to thirty.

"Wait a second," said Cooper.

"What?"

"What about Louisiana?"

"What about it?" asked Soojin.

"Doyle is from Louisiana. Everyone, myself and law enforcement included, has been focused on finding Nash, but what about Doyle?"

"It's a valid question."

"I mean, we all know Doyle helped with the kidnapping, but we assumed he skipped town while Nash took Gabby on the run. But, what if they reconnected in Louisiana? Or maybe Doyle went to Mexico and set everything up for Nash in Louisiana. Coming from a cattle ranch in Texas, Nash doesn't strike me as the kind of guy that would visit Louisiana. And that would fit with what Greene said about it being a location Nash had never visited."

Soojin's eyes lit up. "That's right, remember when I was talking to Nickels at the bar up in Williston?"

Cooper laughed. "How could I forget, Ms. Taekwondo?"

"Nickels talked about Doyle. He said he thought Doyle went back to the bayou in Louisiana."

"Did Nickels give a specific city or location in Louisiana?" asked Cooper.

"Houma?" Soojin rubbed her forehead as she thought back to the conversation she had with Nickels. "I'm pretty sure it was Houma." Soojin perked up. "That could be a good starting place. We could go down there and ask around and see if we can find his houseboat."

"When would we go, though?" asked Cooper. "I mean, Christmas is four days away, and this is all just a guess."

"An educated guess," said Soojin. "We can use the holiday as free time off to help find Gabby. It's not fair to think about where or how she might be spending Christmas this week."

132

Cooper took a drink and looked away as his shoulders dropped. "You know, I hate to say it, but there is a possibility Gabby is—"

Soojin put her drink down. "Don't you dare say it. I'm not ready to give up on her yet. We are going to find her." She blinked back tears.

Cooper put his hand on hers. "No one's giving up. I just don't want to get our hopes up too high."

They both sat there in silence staring at their drinks for a few moments. "Okay," said Cooper. "Let's head to the airport first thing in the morning and see if we can get a flight."

"Thanks." Soojin nodded. "Now, it's time to head over to our big dinner with the governor."

"Ah yes, dinner with North Dakota's governor. Never thought I would cross that one off of my bucket list."

***

It was only a two-block walk from JL Beers to the Pirogue Grille restaurant, but the cold weather made it feel like twenty. Cooper pulled his jacket closer around him as the wind picked up. He wanted a smoke, but he knew that wasn't going to happen. He and Soojin rounded the corner and found the restaurant.

But when they got there, the exterior lights were turned off, and the window blinds were down.

"Is it closed?" asked Soojin.

"That's a good question," said Cooper. "Let me try to look inside."

Cooper stepped up to the main entrance, peering through the glass door. He spotted a light on in the back of the restaurant. "There's someone coming."

Soojin paced back and forth to fight off the cold. "Who is it?"

"Not sure," said Cooper. "Looks like he is wearing a chef's uniform."

"That's weird."

"Really weird."

The chef came to the front door and unlocked it.

"Are you the Smiths?" asked the chef.

"Yes, we are here to see the governor," said Soojin.

"Hello, and welcome to the Pirogue Grille." The chef ushered them in. A lock clicked behind them.

"Thank you," said Cooper.

"Yes, of course. Please follow me." The chef turned and motioned for them to follow. "I'm the owner and head chef. I opened the place at the governor's request for your dinner tonight. I hope you enjoy."

"That's very nice," said Soojin. "Thank you."

They followed him to a private dining area in the back of the restaurant. Two men sat inside drinking and talking, and they stood when Cooper and Soojin entered.

"Mr. and Mrs. Smith, it's so nice to meet both of you. My name is Rick Simmons, and this is my Lieutenant Governor Nate Thompson." Simmons gestured toward Thompson.

"It's a pleasure to meet you too, Mr. Governor," said Cooper. The two men shook hands.

"Thanks for having us here for dinner," said Soojin.

The governor took Soojin's hand and kissed it. "The pleasure is all mine. And please, no titles tonight. Call me Rick, and call that handsome devil Nate."

Did the governor really just kiss Soojin's hand? That's weird.

"Sounds good," said Cooper. He and Soojin shook hands with Nate.

Rick motioned for them to sit down. "Please, take a load off. Can I get you a drink?"

"Not for me," said Soojin. "I'm driving tonight."

"I'll have whatever you gentlemen are drinking."

"Are you sure you don't want a drink?" Nate looked at Soojin. "You know the governor can just tell the state patrol to take the rest of the night off."

Everyone laughed.

"That's quite all right, but thank you," said Soojin.

Rick grabbed a bottle of scotch on the table and poured a glass for Cooper.

"Thank you." Cooper took the drink. "You didn't have to go through the trouble of having the chef open up the restaurant for us on his off day."

"It's not a problem at all," said Rick. "Besides, he owes me a few favors." He winked at Soojin.

Cooper shifted in his seat uncomfortably.

Rick leaned back in his chair. "Plus, I heard you two caused quite the scene up at one of the bars in Williston not too long ago. I wanted to make sure there weren't any witnesses here in case you started kicking us." Rick let out a long laugh.

Soojin turned red. "Sorry about that, we didn't—"

"No need to explain." Rick waved her off. "Besides, those roughnecks need a good whooping once in the while, right?"

"We didn't mean to cause any trouble," said Cooper.

"Forget about it, let's pretend it didn't happen," said Rick.

With the tension in the room cut, everyone began to relax into their chairs, settling in for the evening.

"Now, I'm sure you're wondering why we invited you to dinner," said Nate.

Cooper and Soojin nodded.

Nate set his glass down. "The governor and I wanted to express our sincere thanks and appreciation for all the work the two of you have done to try to bring back our dear Gabby. I'm from Williston, and I watched Gabby grow up. I'll be damned if some roughnecks are going to come in and take her from us."

"And Senator Hanson." Rick shook his head. "The poor senator has been through so much that I just—well, quite frankly, we just need to get her back safely."

"We couldn't agree with you more," said Cooper.

"Gabby and I were good friends," said Soojin. "We had some shared experiences that brought us close, and I just can't bear the thought of her being held against her will. Especially with Christmas coming up in four days."

"Our thoughts exactly," said Nate, nodding. "That is why the governor and I would like to hear any updates you may have on your efforts to find her. We would also like to offer you any additional resources that could help to bring her back."

Cooper took a drink of the whiskey. It burned his throat on the way down. "I just returned from a trip to Texas. I was able to meet with the kidnapper's brother and former partner. Based on those two conversations, and subsequent conversations I've had while updating law enforcement officials, I have an idea of one place they could be."

"Where's that?" asked Rick.

"Louisiana. It could be way off, but it's all we've got right now."

"Hmm . . . Louisiana." Rick rubbed his chin. "I'll be the first to admit there isn't much we can do for her outside of the state, but if she is in North Dakota we can continue to throw more state resources into the search efforts to help find her."

"Everything I've discovered so far leads me to believe they left your state the night Gabby was kidnapped," said Cooper.

"Do you think you'll head down to Louisiana after Christmas?" asked Nate.

Soojin shook her head. "That's too long to wait. We are going to try to leave tomorrow if we can get a flight."

"Those travel expenses will add up quickly," said Rick. He leaned toward Cooper. "Why don't you let us help cover the costs of these trips?"

Cooper blinked in surprise. "Really?"

Rick nodded. "Yes, of course. It's the least we can do."

If he picks up the tab at least that will keep Wild Bill off my back about the expenses.

"That would help out a lot," said Cooper. "We would appreciate it."

"I'll make sure to let Senator Hanson know all of the support you are providing us," said Soojin.

Nate waved her off. "Thanks, but you don't have to do that. I talk to him regularly and I'll make sure he knows everything we've discussed tonight. Have you talked to him recently?"

"I called him yesterday," said Soojin. "He's trying to put on a good face, but you can hear the strain in his voice. I think he's getting depressed with everything that has happened with Gabby and Sydney. And it's probably even harder with Christmas approaching."

Rick turned to Cooper. "Have you met the senator yet?"

"Yes, I met him once at his house before heading down to Texas."

"Did you have a good conversation?"

Why is he so interested in the minutiae of our interactions with the senator? Cooper wondered.

"It was a nice visit, but I know he is busy with his search efforts, and it was a quick meeting."

"I see," said Rick. "And, you're a reporter for MPR out of Saint Paul, right?"

"That's correct."

"How is your story going? Are you working on a piece about North Dakota?"

"I was supposed to work on a story about the oil industry along the Bakken, but that story got derailed when I found out Gabby was kidnapped."

Nate folded his hands on the table, his face composed into an expression of sympathy. "Yes, of course." But then he pressed forward. "So, you're not working on any stories right now?"

"I guess not," said Cooper. "Just trying to focus on Gabby."

Rick and Nate both nodded. "You two are very good friends," said Rick. "I know you'll bring Gabby back safe and sound."

Nate lifted his glass. "A toast to Cooper and Soojin. May you have success in getting our dear Gabby back home soon."

"You can just toast with your water glass." Rick winked at Soojin.

The four of them clanged their glasses together and drank.

"Governor," said Soojin, "you had mentioned you wanted to give a gift to Governor Knutson?"

"Yes, of course. I almost forgot." Rick walked over to the corner of the room and grabbed a large rectangle-shaped item that had a canvas covering it. "Well first of all, please send my regards and congratulate him on his successful reelection campaign."

"I will," said Soojin. "Governor Knutson wanted to congratulate you as well on your successful reelection."

Rick smiled before he pulled the canvas off the gift with a flourish, revealing a painting of a bison stomping the guts out of a gopher on the North Dakota prairie. "After the NDSU Bison football team beat your Minnesota Gophers in a historic game a few years ago, I commissioned a local artist to paint this picture. She is a very talented artist, and she painted two originals for me. I have one hanging at home, and the other one is for your governor. What do you think?"

Soojin forced a smiled. "I think the governor will get a good laugh out of it."

"I knew he would." Rick put the canvas back on and handed it to Soojin.

"I'm sure Governor Knutson will return the favor soon," she said.

"Bring it on," said Rick. "I'll be here for at least four more years."

They all laughed.

"Okay, now back to business before the food gets here," said Nate.

"Yes, back to business," echoed Rick.

"The Hanson family is going through a very stressful time right now, as you can imagine," said Nate. "I know Mark and Sydney have a lot going through their heads, and Sydney has her ongoing health issues. If they ask either one of you for anything, and I mean *anything*, please just come directly to me with the request. Here is my number." Nate handed Cooper his card.

"That is great," said Cooper. "Is it okay to let the senator know you're helping us out?"

"We would prefer to be anonymous," Rick said. "You know, Senator Hanson is a proud man, and he's never asked for help before. He also gets things confused sometimes."

"What do you mean?" asked Cooper.

Rick leaned in closer. "Please keep this between us, but it's possible the Senator has some sort of health issue."

"Could be something like the early stages of Alzheimer's," said Nate, "although he's always been one for making up stories."

"Yeah," agreed Rick. "These days, you can never tell if he is making something up or if he just truly doesn't remember. It's a shame really, with Sydney not being in much of a position to help keep him on track."

Cooper nodded for show, but his mind was full of doubts. *What do they think, I'm like ten years old? Why are they trying to discredit the senator?*

"Thanks for the heads up," said Cooper. "I'll keep it in mind."

Cooper glanced at Soojin. Her face revealed nothing, but he knew she was probably wondering why the governor was trying to discredit the senator.

"Okay, okay, enough about business," said Rick. "It's time to eat."

"What's on the menu?" asked Soojin.

Rick grinned wickedly. "Deep-fried gopher. Just how we like 'em here in North Dakota."

CHAPTER 19

The Louisiana Bayou

The rain continued to pelt the top of the houseboat as Nash grew more impatient with each passing hour. He was still reeling from Gabby's recent attempt to escape. Now, he sat in the corner of the living room watching her sleep on the couch, her leg securely chained to the table once more.

I thought we were getting somewhere, Nash thought. *She was just playing with my emotions. How could I be so stupid? She'll never love me.*

Nash had felt this way once before—after he had called off the wedding with his former fiancée. He later regretted his decision, but by then she was long gone.

He took out a piece of paper.

MY BIGGEST REGRETS:
1. Fumbling away our high school state football championship
2. Not being able to save fallen fellow soldiers in Iraq
3. Throwing away my first love
4. Refusing to take medicine for my problem
5. Getting kicked out of the Rangers
6. Cutting off communication with my parents before they died
7. Moving to North Dakota (Gabby messed up my mind and future)

Nash knew he would have to wait out the torrential downpour if he were to have any chance getting back to Houma. He hoped it would die down before Christmas Eve, because that was when he planned to make his move. Law enforcement and border patrol would be lax on Christmas Eve and Day. He would drive through the night all the way to Key West. From there, he knew a guy who could take him by sailboat down to Cancun. Once in Mexico, he could easily bounce around the massive country, or move farther into Latin America.

The only question is, do I take the girl or leave her here?

Just then, Gabby turned over and stretched. She looked over at Nash.

"Mind if I use the bathroom quick?" she asked.

"Sure." Nash bent to unlock her chain. As he did, she lightly squeezed his arm. Not just any squeeze, but the kind a woman gives a man to make him feel as though he has won her heart. Nash burned inside, going completely still.

Gabby met his eyes. "Declan, I'm really sorry about what happened yesterday. I—I just don't know what came over me. I didn't mean to cause you any harm, and I wanted to say thanks for saving my life."

Nash didn't know how to respond, so he just nodded and finished unlocking the chain. She let go of his arm and walked past him to the bathroom, shutting the door behind her.

How can a woman cause such desire in my heart with just one touch and comment, when minutes before I condemned her?

He didn't know what he would do next.

Well, I could bring her. Why not?

Nash started pacing the houseboat's living room.

On the other hand, she could be playing me like the used trombone I am.

He would ask her a few questions to gauge her willingness to go along with him. If she was against it, that would be the end of it. If she went along with it, then they might still have a future.

Gabby came out of the bathroom and headed back toward the couch. She sat down and started putting the chain around her ankle.

"Wait," said Nash. "Not right now. Can we talk?"

"Of course." Gabby looked up at Nash.

She looks like an angel, and those eyes melt me.

Nash sat down across from her. "How do you feel about coming with me on the next leg of this journey?"

Gabby averted her gaze. Then she looked right back into Nash's eyes and said, "I think it would be a good idea to move on together to the next destination. This spot isn't safe."

Nash's heart started to beat faster. He had butterflies in his stomach. It was as if he was in high school all over again asking a popular girl to the prom.

"That's great to hear, miss—"

"Just call me Gabby, I'm tired of all the 'miss' talk. It's too formal for this northern girl." Gabby smiled.

Nash laughed. *She broke the ice, we are all good again!*

"Okay, thanks. I agree, we've been here too long. I'd like to leave sooner, but there is no way we are getting anywhere in this rainstorm. Especially in that canoe. My new plan is to leave on Christmas Eve, since it'll be a quiet day to travel."

"Where are we headed next?"

He bit his lip. "How do you feel about Mexico?"

Gabby slowly nodded. "Mexico is good. I think it's a logical place to head next."

Nash smiled. "Perfect, then that's where we will go. We should be safe there. Well, as long as we don't get into the drug trafficking business."

Gabby laughed. "How will we get there?"

"Leave those details to me. Just rest up, because we'll be leaving in two days and it may be a long and exhausting trip."

"Do you speak any Spanish?"

"Enough to get us by. You?"

"*Si, hablo espanol.*"

Wow, and she speaks Spanish? This girl is the whole package. Even better than I dreamed.

"*Muy bien!* We will be able to get around just fine down there. What a pleasant early Christmas gift." Nash blushed.

She gazed into his eyes. "*Feliz Navidad.*"

He melted back into his chair.

We will be together forever.

CHAPTER 20

Williston, North Dakota

There were no flights down to Louisiana out of Bismarck, but there was a late-night flight to Houston out of Williston. Cooper and Soojin booked the flight to Houston, with an early morning connection to New Orleans. From there, they could rent a car and drive the rest of the way to Houma.

It was a three-and-a-half-hour drive from Bismarck to Williston with nothing to look at but oil drills and flat prairie land covered in snow. Even though their flight was late in the day, they got an early start so they could stop by the repair shop to check on Cooper's Jeep before they headed to the airport.

"Was it just me, or was that kind of weird last night with the governor and lieutenant governor?" asked Soojin.

"It was really strange," said Cooper. "That governor is a horn ball; he was totally checking you out all night."

Soojin scrunched up her face in disgust. "And what was all that talk about Senator Hanson and his health, and about him fabricating stories? I've known him for years, and he has never made anything up. His mind is sharp."

"They were trying to discredit Senator Hanson for some reason." Cooper looked over at Soojin as she drove. "Wait a second, do you think it's possible this has something to do with the big story Mark told me he would share after we find Gabby?"

Soojin glanced at Cooper before returning her attention to the road. "It's possible. We can ask Mark this afternoon when we leave the vehicles at his place."

Cooper nodded. "I think I will. I'd also like to see if he has any other updates on Gabby before we head down south."

They arrived in Williston around lunchtime, and Soojin took Cooper directly to the auto repair shop. Wellstone was parked on the edge of the lot, and at first glance it looked pretty good. Cooper jumped out of the rental car and went up to his beloved Jeep, sliding his hand across the hood. He popped it open and checked the engine. Everything looked right. He knelt down underneath the vehicle to check the frame, impressed by how straight it was now. Cooper nodded in approval, and then went into the shop to pay and get his keys.

Come on buddy, start for me.

The temperature was hovering around thirty-two degrees, so Cooper wasn't expecting any problem with the battery. It took a second to turn over, but then it was firing on all cylinders.

Back from the dead, it's a miracle.

Cooper smiled and waved at Soojin. She was off to the Hanson residence to check up on Sydney. Cooper would join them once Mark was home, but first he had a lunch meeting with Lisa Larson, at Bill Anderson's request.

Lisa agreed to meet him at a place called Gramma Sharon's Family Restaurant, located just off of Highway 2. Cooper took the opportunity to smoke a cigarette as he pulled Wellstone into the parking lot. As he finished his smoke he looked over and saw there was a green Volkswagen beetle already parked by the front door. It had Wisconsin vanity plates that read *Larson.*

Oh jeez, here we go. The last time he saw her car was in the MPR parking lot. She had cut him off one morning and took the last open spot.

Cooper flicked his cigarette out and walked into the restaurant. He immediately saw Lisa's blazing red glasses across the diner. She was sitting in a booth by the windows, typing away on her laptop, headphones in her ears. She didn't look up when Cooper sat down across from her.

A waitress offered Cooper a cup of coffee, and he ordered a grilled ham and cheese sandwich. The waitress then turned her attention to Lisa, who slowly took her headphones off.

"I'll just have a caramel roll," said Lisa. "No coffee."

The waitress took the menus and walked away. Lisa finally looked over and acknowledged Cooper's presence.

"Hello, Lisa." Cooper smiled.

"Hello, Cooper." Lisa's own smile was forced.

"Good to see you are as chipper here as you are back home. How are you enjoying your time in North Dakota?"

Lisa shrugged. "I can't complain. While you are out chasing a wild goose, I'm here getting a real story about what's going on in the Bakken. So I want to thank you, for handing me the position on the investigative team."

Cooper sighed. "Finding Gabby matters more to me than any story or promotion."

"And the longer you try to find her, the closer I am to my promotion."

"Seriously, what have you been working on?" pressed Cooper. "I know Wild Bill wanted us to connect so we could try to work as a team. Did you hear any more about that flash fire in Watford City?"

Lisa looked down at her laptop. "Yes, I interviewed someone who was there the night of the fire, and others who have worked there. Sounds like that drill did not require the men to wear flame-resistant clothing. But, the lead driller that night, the one flown to Regions in Saint Paul—"

"Marshall?" Cooper interrupted.

Lisa looked up and shot Cooper a look. "Yes, Marshall. Do you want to hear my story or what?"

"Yes, sorry, please go on."

"So, Marshall told everyone to put their FRCs on anyway, but they wouldn't listen. I guess it's like asking a grown man to wear his seatbelt in the car. He either is going to do it, or he's not. So, when the flash fire came up only Marshall had his FRC on. Did you know the flame that comes up could be up to nineteen-hundred degrees Fahrenheit and last up to five seconds?"

"No, but five seconds at that temperature would feel like an eternity with or without FRCs," said Cooper.

"The FRC was the only reason Marshall survived," Lisa said. "The other roughneck on the drill wasn't wearing them, and he's dead now."

"Brutal." Cooper sipped his coffee. Then he asked, "What's the deal with the oil spill?"

"It's pretty bad," said Lisa. "About three million gallons of wastewater have spilled out into the area. It's already destroyed a creek and surrounding farmland. One farmer I talked to had oil seeping up through the snow in his backyard."

"Jeez, that's unbelievable."

The food arrived, and Lisa started typing again while Cooper ate.

"What are you working on now?"

"I'm transcribing an interview I had this morning with a young woman here in Williston." Lisa turned her laptop around so it faced Cooper. "Read the highlighted text."

I live in a 250-square-foot apartment. Certain groceries are a luxury for me, if I can get them at all. I carry mace with me everywhere I go, and never stay out after dark. My life as a single woman in western North Dakota is so different from where I was born and raised in Moorhead, Minnesota.

"Dang," said Cooper. "Well, I hate to admit it, but looks like you are getting some solid interviews."

"Hey, listen." Lisa leaned in closer. "Something weird is going on out here."

"What do you mean?"

"I think I'm being followed."

The hair on the back of Cooper's neck rose. "What makes you think that?"

"I've seen the same guy around town a few times, and I've spotted a recurring vehicle in different places. But what's even more strange is I've been stopped three times on the highways by the state troopers."

"Were you speeding?"

"Not really, but they give me two warnings and one speeding ticket for going seven miles per hour over. I haven't been pulled over in any state for years, and certainly never given a ticket for going seven over."

"They were state troopers every time?"

"Yes, all three. Different ones, too."

"Who supervises the state troopers?" asked Cooper.

Lisa paused. "I think it's the governor. Why?"

Cooper shifted uncomfortably. "I don't know, it just seems like maybe there is someone who is purposely making your stay in North Dakota a little more difficult than it needs to be. Perhaps you are getting close to something that someone doesn't want you to know about. I'm not saying it was the governor, but who else could tell three different state troopers to pull you over?"

"I don't know, but I don't like it." Lisa took a bite of her caramel roll.

Cooper took that as an invitation to finish his sandwich.

"It's interesting you thought you were being followed." Cooper scanned the diner to see if anyone was looking at them, then lowered his voice. "When I was down in Texas, I thought the same thing. I can't say for sure, but I believe there was a vehicle following me as I went from place to place looking for clues about the kidnapper."

"Any idea who it could have been?" asked Lisa.

Cooper shook his head. "It doesn't make any sense to me. Why would someone be following me in Texas?"

"Not sure," said Lisa. "Say, I'm just going to wrap up a few more interviews here and then head back to Wisconsin for Christmas."

"Well, I'll be around the rest of the afternoon in case something comes up," said Cooper. "But I'm heading down to Houston tonight, and Louisiana tomorrow morning, so I'll be gone for a few days."

Lisa looked up from her laptop and smiled the smile of a chess player who knew she had her opponent in checkmate. "Good luck with that," she said sarcastically, then put her headphones back in.

"Thanks a million."

***

Cooper slowed Wellstone down on the highway heading out of Williston and turned his signal light on for the turn into the Hanson driveway. As he neared it, a black vehicle pulled out and turned away from him. It had the unmistakable taillights of a Dodge Charger.

For Pete's sake, what is with this car? First Texas, now here?

Then he remembered where else he had seen a black Dodge Charger—when he met that private investigator at Hanson's house.

But why would he follow me all the way to Texas?

Cooper parked next to Soojin's vehicle. Popping a piece of licorice into his mouth, he smelled his jacket to make sure the cigarette scent wasn't too strong. Then he went up to the front door. Once again, Senator Hanson opened it before Cooper could knock.

"Hello, Cooper. Great to see you again." Mark gave Cooper a firm handshake.

"Nice to see you again too, senator. I hope you and Sydney are doing okay."

"Come on in out of the cold." Mark slapped Cooper's back as he pulled him inside.

The scent of freshly baked goods wafted into the entryway. Cooper took a deep breath. "It smells wonderful in here."

"Syd normally bakes her world-famous annual Christmas cookies, but because of her health I took a stab at making them this year. I wasn't going to make them with Gabby being gone, but Syd convinced me to do it anyway so you and Soojin could enjoy a treat with us before you head out on your trip."

Cooper took his coat off, and Mark hung it up on a hook. "That's really nice; you didn't have to do that."

Mark waved him into the living room. "Not a problem. Come on in and join us."

The two men walked into the living room, where Soojin and Sydney sat talking on the couch. A fire was lit, and a few Christmas lights hung over the fireplace, but Cooper guessed it was less festive than usual considering the circumstances. He couldn't even spot a Christmas tree or any stockings.

Sydney looked pale and fragile as she sat close to the fireplace. Cooper could only imagine the toll her body had taken from the cancer and rounds of treatment.

"Hello, Cooper." Sydney waved to greet him. "Please, have a seat. Care for some hot apple cider and Christmas cookies?"

"That would be wonderful, thank you." Cooper waved and smiled at Soojin, but she didn't return it. Her face was drawn.

When Sydney turned to say something to Mark, Cooper gave Soojin a puzzled look. *Are you mad at me?* he mouthed.

From the couch, Sydney asked, "Soojin do you care for any more?"

"Yes, please," Soojin said, ignoring Cooper's question.

What the heck did I do now? he wondered.

Sydney motioned for Mark to grab the drinks and desserts. Mark reached for a tray on a nearby table with a mug of hot cider and two plates of Christmas cookies. He handed the mug and one plate to Cooper, and the other to Soojin.

"Thank you so much," said Cooper. "Looks delicious."

"Yes, thank you," said Soojin.

"They're not too bad for his first-ever attempt at making Christmas cookies." Sydney started to laugh but covered her mouth as she broke into a muffled cough.

Mark sat down next to Cooper on the other couch. "So, are you guys ready for your trip down to Louisiana? Is there anything else we can do to help?"

"We should be good," said Soojin.

Cooper shifted his attention from Soojin to Mark. "Thanks for letting us leave our vehicles here, and for offering to drive us to the airport tonight."

"It's not a problem," said Mark. "You guys are our best hope of finding Gabby. We are getting nowhere with law enforcement. They keep talking about limited resources, and the low percent chance of ever finding her again given the number of days she has been gone. Plus, with the holiday all efforts have basically stopped."

"That's terrible," said Soojin. "You would think your pull with the city and state elected officials would get you more resources."

Mark stroked his chin, gazing into the fireplace. "Well, I think Governor Simmons was behind sending that private investigator, Wheeler. I know he offered to help, but he's not known for his *pro bono* work. Plus, he's worked on cases with the governor in the past, so it only makes sense."

"Did he just leave your house driving the Dodge Charger?" asked Cooper.

"Yes," said Mark. "He didn't have much of anything for me, other than to say he has been doing some traveling to see if he can help chase down some leads on Gabby."

Before taking a bite of a cookie, Cooper looked over at Soojin. When she wouldn't meet his eyes, he turned back toward Mark. "Did Wheeler say where he went?"

"He went down to Texas," said Mark. "He refuses to fly, so he complained about the long drive."

A sweat began to break out on Cooper's skin. Ignoring it, he bit into a cookie. "This is delicious," he told Mark. "I never would have known it was your first time." Cooper winked at Sydney.

Sydney forced a smile, and her hands shook as she reached for the cookie tray. "I'm glad they turned out okay."

Cooper returned his attention to Mark. "Say, do you know when Wheeler left on his last trip, and how long he was gone?"

Mark narrowed his eyes as he thought. "I guess he left about a week ago, and he just got back these past few days."

The timing checks out. Something smells like lutefisk here.

"If you don't mind me asking," said Cooper, "how well do you know Governor Simmons and Lieutenant Governor Thompson?"

Mark readjusted himself in his seat. "Probably a little better than I wish I did. Why do you ask?"

"I don't know if Soojin told you, but we met with the two of them last night in Bismarck at a restaurant. They invited us to dinner to ask about how the search for Gabby was going, and Governor Simmons also gave Soojin a gift to give to Governor Knutson."

Mark's gaze on Cooper became intent. "What else did they say?"

Soojin cut in. "It was the strangest thing. They were talking about you, and telling us how you make up stories, and that you were having health issues. I know that's not true, though. Why would they say that?"

Mark glanced over at Sydney, but her eyes were trained on her mug of cider. "Those rotten, no good . . ." Mark let his voice trail off as he clenched his teeth. Then he composed himself and looked back at Cooper.

"Do you remember when I told you I wanted to give you a story after you found Gabby?"

Cooper set his plate of cookies down. "Yes, of course."

"Well, I won't go into the details, but it involves both of them. They know what I know about them, and they clearly want to discredit me."

Mark patted Cooper on the shoulder. "I won't lie, my hands aren't totally clean, either," he said. "The governor knows that. When you've been in politics for as long as I have, you end up with some skeletons in your closet."

"Yeah, but what—"

Mark waved Cooper off. "Go find Gabby, and we will arrange a time when we can meet and I can give you a story that will make waves across our state and beyond."

"Okay. I'll wait until then." Cooper nodded, then noticed that Soojin was glaring at him. Cooper's eyes widened.

"Cooper," said Soojin, "can you run outside and grab my bags out of the trunk of my car? I want to transfer some of the items from my suitcase into the carry-on bag so we can get through the airports faster on our trip."

"Sure," said Cooper.

Anything to stop you from being mad at me.

"You can use the guest room to sort your items," said Sydney.

"Thank you," said Soojin.

Cooper didn't bother to grab his coat on the way out the door. Bracing himself against the cold, he ran out and popped Soojin's trunk, grabbed the two bags, and hurried back inside.

"The guest room is the last door down the hallway on the right-hand side," said Mark from the living room.

"Perfect, thanks," said Cooper.

Soojin was standing in the middle of the guest room when Cooper got there. She held his jacket in one arm, his pack of American Spirit cigarettes in the other.

Holy Hannah.

"What are these?"

Cooper felt his face get hot. "I can explain."

"No, you can't. You smelled like a chimney the second you walked into the Hanson living room, and you've been smoking behind my back ever since we returned from Europe."

Cooper knew not to test the limits of her patience. "Soojin, I'm sorry—"

She stopped him with a cold stare before he could go on. "No, this is not okay with me. You are quitting smoking right now, or we are spending Christmas apart."

Cooper's shoulders drooped.

"Cooper Smith. You are better than this." She threw down his jacket and tossed the cigarettes into the trash can. "Do you want to die of lung cancer?"

"Of course not. Things have been a little tense lately, and I've been using them to calm my nerves."

"Well, it stops tonight. Get the gum or the patch or whatever you need, but no husband of mine is going to smoke. That goes for cigars, too."

Cooper put his head in his hands and rubbed his temples, dreading the nicotine withdrawals he would have to face. It would be just like the last time he quit smoking cold turkey three years before. He had just left a job working for a local television station in his hometown of Duluth. He had hated that job, where all he'd done was cover high school sports at his *alma mater*. Then he found a job as a reporter for a popular news radio program in Duluth, and used it as an opportunity to start fresh. The tedium and unhappiness of his previous position had him smoking more than ever before, so he decided the new position would be the perfect opportunity to adopt a healthier lifestyle. Plus, giving up smoking might improve his radio voice. The focus at his new job paid off, since that experience helped him land his role as a reporter for MPR.

His hands slid down his face before he put his palms together in a praying gesture under his chin, looking up at Soojin. She had her hands on her hips.

Why was I willing to give up smoking when I started a new career three years ago only to start smoking again so soon after getting married? Soojin is worth so much more to me than careers and cigarettes.

Cooper hung his head. "Cold turkey it is."

"Good." Soojin gave Cooper one quick nod of her head as if the matter was put to bed forever. "Now, let's go find Gabby."

CHAPTER 21

Houma, Louisiana

After a late-night flight from Williston to Houston, and an early morning connection to New Orleans, Cooper and Soojin picked up a rental vehicle and drove the rest of the way to Houma. There were literally two vehicles left at the Hertz car rental kiosk at the airport that morning, so they opted to go with the Nissan Quest minivan over the Mustang convertible, which cost twice as much. They rolled into Houma in a silver soccer mom van just after 10 am two days before Christmas.

We just need some screaming toddlers and a barking puppy to get the full minivan experience, thought Cooper.

Their plan was to visit the docks and marinas near Houma that accommodated houseboats to see if they could find Brock Doyle's. With each new stop, Cooper and Soojin gleaned more information from the locals who would highlight additional marinas that may dock houseboats.

Cooper felt another nicotine-withdrawal headache coming on. He was eating licorice nonstop, and munching on Juicy Fruit chewing gum—three pieces at a time—between bags. He was also starting to get irritable.

"Maybe this is all a big waste of time," he barked at Soojin as he drove.

She glanced up from her phone, where she was following Google Maps to the next marina. "Hold it together; it's been what, one day since you gave up smoking?"

Cooper smacked down on his gum. "I'm being serious. What if she isn't even here? We could just be wasting our time."

"Just keep chewing your gum and drive," Soojin said.

Cooper fumed. *Easy for you to say; you've never tried to quit smoking.*

"Turn left at the next stop sign," said Soojin. "Then, it's the first road on the right. Should be called Leroy's Landing."

When Cooper turned down the designated road, he saw a worn-down sign that read, *Leroy's Landing: Fairly Reliable Fish Guide and Dock Services.*

This should be interesting.

After growing up in northern Minnesota, Cooper felt incredibly culture-shocked in Texas and Louisiana. He took notice of the slow Southern drawl, the sweet tea and barbeque, the hot and sunny weather, the jazz and blues music, the cowboy boots and deserts in Texas, and the shrimp boots and swamps in Louisiana. In Minnesota it was Scandinavian phrases like *uffda mayda*, coffee and Tater Tot hotdish, cold and dark weather, Bob Dylan and Prince, Red Wing boots and lakes.

Cooper slapped his neck after a mosquito bit into him. He pulled his hand away and saw it was covered in blood. *Well, I guess the north and the south have that in common,* he thought.

Cooper wiped his hand on his pant leg as he pulled the minivan up to what looked like the marina's office. Beyond a cluster of small buildings, he could see a series of docks with several boats tied to them, including what looked like houseboats. The skies were clear, and it was a comfortable sixty-five degrees. But the air was heavy and the water was high following a recent rainstorm. The local radio news had been talking about the storm for the past hour. And although people back home in Minnesota could talk about the weather all day long, Cooper finally had enough and turned the radio off.

He exited the minivan and walked around to the office door. Soojin was already knocking and waiting for a response. Cooper peered into the windows.

"Hello?" she said. "Is anyone here?"

Cooper saw a door at the back of the office open, and a short, black man with a cane hobbled to the front of the building. He unlocked the door, swinging it open. He wore a tattered baseball hat with a fishing lure sticking out of it and a shirt that read, *Leroy's Landing: EST 1971.*

"Can I help you?" he asked.

"We hope so," said Soojin. "Are you the owner of this marina?"

"Sure am; I'm Leroy. Been running this place for forty-three years now." Leroy pointed to his shirt. "What can I do you for?"

He had a thick Southern drawl, and a couple of his lower teeth were missing.

"Great, we've come to the right man," said Soojin. "We are just wondering if there is a houseboat docked at your marina that is owned by a man named Brock Doyle."

Leroy raised his eyebrows. "You guys know Doyle?"

Cooper's bad mood immediately lifted as excitement coursed through him. "Wait, do *you* know Doyle?"

"Well, sure. What do you want with him?"

Soojin jumped in. "We are trying to find him because we have a few questions we hope he can answer for us. It's very important."

Leroy shrugged. "Come on in and have a seat."

Cooper and Soojin exchanged relieved glances as they walked into Leroy's office.

"I've got some Abita's beer in the fridge." Leroy motioned to an old fridge in the corner. "Or, if you prefer a soft drink I think I also have a few Abita's vanilla cream sodas."

The office was small, with two windows and an overhead fan that was spinning directly above them. Pictures of Leroy with happy clients who had caught big fish, presumably on one of his guiding tours, lined the walls. An old metal desk sat in the center of the room, with two visitor chairs facing it. Leroy limped behind his desk and sat down, but Cooper and Soojin remained standing.

"Thanks for the drink offer, but I'm okay," said Cooper.

"Me too," said Soojin. "We're sorry to burst in here unexpectedly, but we really would like to speak with Doyle. Do you know where we can find him?"

Leroy laughed. "Good luck with that."

"What do you mean?" asked Cooper.

"Well, I'm assuming he is still up in the Dakotas doing his oil gig, so you've got a ways to go." Leroy paused and scratched his head. "Then again, about two weeks ago I did my daily checks on the boats in the marina. Doyle's boat was gone. I'm not surprised; he always comes in unannounced at all hours of the night, takes out his houseboat and heads out to the bayou to go off the grid for a while. Sometimes he is gone for a month at a time. Of course, it could have been a friend or someone else that took it. Who knows with that guy ..." Leroy shrugged.

"That's a long time to be out on the bayou, isn't it?" asked Soojin.

Even though they had yet to see anyone else in the whole marina, Leroy glanced out the window before he leaned in closer to Cooper and Soojin. He held his right hand up alongside his mouth and whispered, "The only time he ever makes quick trips is when he is paying a hustler to go out there to fornicate with him."

Cooper grinned and Soojin shook her head.

"How do you know Doyle, anyway?" asked Leroy.

"We think he might know the whereabouts of a close friend of mine who was recently kidnapped," said Soojin.

"Oh, really …" Leroy said the word *really* for what felt like several seconds too long to Cooper.

"Yes. So if by chance Doyle came back down here from North Dakota, and if he took his boat out into the bayou, do you think you could find him out there?" Cooper motioned beyond the marina to the vast swampland.

Leroy studied them, his hands folded over his belly. After a long, silent minute, he answered. "I have one guess. It's a hideout I showed him a little while back."

"Can you take us there?" asked Soojin.

Leroy shook his head. "Doyle paid me fifty bucks to show him that spot. He said I wasn't allowed to show it to anyone else."

"Sir, this is really important," said Cooper.

Leroy put his hand up by his mouth to whisper again. "I think that is the exact spot he uses for his fornication."

"We'll pay you one-hundred bucks right now to show us that spot," said Soojin. "And, we will pay Doyle fifty when we get there so he doesn't feel slighted by you."

"No, no, no." Leroy held up his hands. "I couldn't possibly do that. Besides, it's too far to go and come back before dark, and it's nasty out there. A ton of mosquitos, and alligators big enough to eat a whole horse. The water is still too high from the storm. Did you hear about the storm?"

"We'll make it two-hundred," said Soojin.

Leroy considered, then nodded. "Come back early tomorrow morning and I'll bring you there."

"Can't wait," said Cooper.

CHAPTER 22

Bismarck, North Dakota

A familiar evening unfolded in the governor's private office at his residence. Simmons relaxed in his chair, his feet up on his desk. Thompson reclined in a chair on the other side of the table. Both men were enjoying a glass of whiskey. The room was dark, except for a few dimly lit lamps and a withering flame in the fireplace.

"Tomorrow is Christmas Eve," said Simmons. "Whaddya say we turn on some Christmas tunes?"

"Sounds good to me," said Thompson.

Simmons sat up in his chair, set his glass down on the desk, and grabbed a remote control. He pointed it to a CD player across the room and clicked play. Bing Crosby started to croon about having a white Christmas. Simmons set the remote down and opened one of his desk doors, pulling out two cigars, a cutter, and a lighter.

"And, because I'm in such a festive mood, I'd like to share a Cuban cigar with my lieutenant." Simmons cut both cigars and handed one to Thompson. After lighting his, Simmons threw Thompson the lighter.

"Well, that sure is kind of you," said Thompson, lighting his cigar. "Thanks. Why are you in such a good mood?"

"'Tis the season to be merry, my friend." Simmons leaned closer and spoke quietly. "I got some action last night from this girl I have on the side. She's wild in bed, and I feel like a college kid again every time I'm with her."

Thompson smiled and took a long pull from his cigar. "Holy smokes. I don't know how you do it with all those women."

Thompson's reply was louder than Simmons would have liked. "Whoa, keep your voice down." Simmons pulled the cigar out of his mouth and put his index finger up to his lips. "I don't want Mrs. Simmons to hear any of this locker-room talk, or I'm sleeping on the couch."

Thompson laughed. "My bad, I'll try to keep it down. Maybe you should just turn Bing Crosby up."

Simmons chuckled. "I'm also happy because that reporter is running around chasing ghosts down in Louisiana, and I think Hanson may have finally cooled down."

"You going to send Wheeler down to Louisiana after Smith?" asked Thompson.

"Nah, no need." Simmons took a puff of his cigar. "First of all, it was pretty clear in Texas that the reporter is getting nowhere in his search. The more time he spends trekking across the countryside looking for the senator's dead granddaughter, the less time he spends chatting up Hanson. Plus, Wheeler refused to do another drive down south after his Texas trip last week. That reminds me, I need to find a new private eye. Someone who will actually fly around to get stuff done."

"You really think Gabby is dead?"

Simmons set his cigar on an ashtray and took a big swig of his whiskey. "I hate to say it, being Christmas and all. But yeah, she's probably buried in some remote stretch of land, never to be found again."

Thompson looked down into his glass and shook his head. "I know you aren't a big fan of Hanson, especially with the way he's waffling on our agreement, but that's kind of hard for me to think about. Being from the same town and all."

"Cheer up, lieutenant. Hanson isn't going to go public with anything until he finds his granddaughter, and with each day, that looks less likely to happen. Plus, it's almost Christmas, and this time of year there are so many desperate housewives looking to please someone in power." Simmons winked. "Someone like yourself."

"Ah, cut it out. You know I'm not into all that."

"I'm just saying, is all. No harm in thinking about it."

"Hey, not to be a downer, but did you see the price of oil just dropped to sixty dollars per barrel? It's down another twenty percent this month."

Simmons waved him off. "That's nothing to worry about; it just means the little oil guys will be cut out and the big boys can take over. Oil always goes back up, you know that."

"Yeah. The state's rainy day fund remains over a billion dollars, and we still have less than three percent unemployment."

Simmons smiled, stood up, and extended his glass out across the table. "There's the glass half-full attitude I was looking for. Now, I would like to make a toast."

Thompson also stood and raised his glass.

"A toast to you, my faithful lieutenant governor, and to me, the man on the throne. May we reign forever!"

Both men laughed as they clinked their glasses.

"You know," said Thompson. "I know you have four more years here on the throne in North Dakota, but have you thought any more about a 2016 presidential run?"

Simmons set his glass down, gazing over at the dying fire. After a few long moments, he turned his attention back to Thompson. "The thought had crossed my mind. Who knows what knuckleheads will run for the GOP nomination in two years? I'm sure I could beat most of them on merit alone."

"You got that right. And if you don't win, who cares? It'll put you on the national stage, and then you come back here and finish out your term and try again in 2020."

Simmons smiled, then looked down at the Nixon bobblehead doll on his desk. "What do you think about that, President Nixon?" Simmons flicked Nixon's head and it nodded up and down in agreement. "Yeah, I agree with you, too."

CHAPTER 23

The Louisiana Bayou

After a restless night, Cooper drove the minivan from the hotel in Houma back to Leroy's Landing early in the morning on Christmas Eve. Cooper tried calling Fletcher on the way to update him on the plan to search for Doyle's houseboat. Fletcher didn't answer, so Cooper settled for leaving him a voicemail.

Not that Fletcher could do anything from way up in North Dakota anyway, thought Cooper.

He parked in front of Leroy's office, and Soojin noticed a note on the door. She ran out and read it, then came back to the minivan and pointed out to the docks. Cooper rolled down the window to talk to her.

"He's out getting a boat ready," said Soojin. "He asked for us to meet him there."

"Sounds good, let's go," said Cooper.

The morning was cool, and an eerie, light fog hung over the swampy water. On the way to the docks, Cooper swallowed a couple Aleve tablets for his withdrawal headache. He had cut back a little on the licorice, but was still chewing gum nonstop. His jaw was starting to get sore, but he popped two more pieces of Juicy Fruit into his mouth for the boat ride anyway.

When they reached the main dock, Leroy was loading up an airboat with supplies.

Hot dang, thought Cooper. *This is going to be wild.*

"Are we really taking an airboat?" Cooper looked over at Soojin excitedly.

She smiled. "Sure looks like it."

"Have you ever been on one?"

"No, this will be my first time."

"Same here."

Leroy stood up and waved. He wore the same clothes as yesterday, with the addition of a jacket. He stood on the front of a silver airboat, with a huge fan, two big strobe lights, a captain's chair mounted up high, and a lower bench. Two metal crates sat at the feet of the bench, which Leroy closed and latched up.

"Who's ready for a tour?" Leroy smiled.

"Are we really taking that thing out?" asked Cooper.

"Of course—it's the only way to get around quickly out on the bayou," said Leroy.

"You know it's Christmas Eve, right?" asked Soojin. "We really appreciate you taking us out; I hope your family isn't too upset."

Leroy shook his head. "I've spent the last forty-three Christmas holidays right here in this marina office watching old Christmas reruns by myself. It'll be nice to have some company for a change."

"Well, this is our first time ever riding on an airboat, so we are at your mercy," said Cooper.

Leroy laughed. "Nothing to it. Jump on down here and get settled."

Soojin crawled in first, and Cooper followed. They sat down on the bench and clicked their lap belts into place. Leroy handed them ear mufflers.

"Once we get going, you're going to need those things or you'll go deaf." Leroy limped over to the rope connecting the boat to the dock and untied it.

"Are you recovering from an injury?" Soojin pointed at Leroy's leg.

Leroy chuckled. "You could say that." He put his foot up on the bench right between Cooper and Soojin, pulling up his pants to reveal a prosthetic leg.

"What happened?" asked Cooper.

"An alligator as big as this boat came up and bit my lower leg clean off. Happened right in the very same waters we are heading to today."

Cooper and Soojin stared up at Leroy. He grinned, rolling his pants back down. "Now would be a good time to put on those ear muffs."

Cooper and Soojin turned to look at each other, their eyes still wide. Soojin mouthed, *YOLO.*

Cooper smiled and gripped his seat with both hands as Leroy started the engine and lurched into the bayou.

Soojin's right, Cooper thought. *You only live once.*

***

They had been paddling the canoe for hours already. Gabby's shoulders ached, but Nash directed her to push on. The quiet and the stillness of the bayou was creeping Gabby out.

Today's your day to get away, she thought, *or you'll be stuck with this guy in the basement of a house in rural Mexico. Never to be seen again.*

Right before they left the houseboat that morning, Gabby had asked to use the bathroom one last time. She made sure Nash had already used it so he would not go in after her. A few days before, she had hid a piece of paper and a pen in the back of a drawer in there. It was still waiting for her. She'd had a lot of time on Nash's couch to craft the perfect message in her head. She left it on the counter near the sink and prayed that someone would find it soon.

Nash grunted behind her as he worked the paddle at the back of the canoe.

"Hey, I know you're tired," he said, his own voice breathless, "but we have to power through this section of water so we can get to the marina."

Gabby put her paddle back into the water. "My arms are burning."

"Okay, let's go behind this patch of cypress trees up ahead and take a five-minute break," Nash said. "I have to look at the map again, anyway."

Gabby was grateful for the chance to rest. The last time she had paddled a canoe was in college, when she and Soojin had gone on a trip up to the Boundary Waters Canoe Area in northern Minnesota. She remembered her arms and shoulders burning on that trip as well, but the scenery and wildlife had made it worth it. She remembered loons calling in the distance as they sat around the campfire chatting about life, politics, and men. Neither of them could have envisioned something like this would happen.

I wonder how Soojin is doing. I bet she had a blast on her honeymoon in Europe.

All of a sudden, the canoe rocked, startling her from her thoughts. When she turned, Nash was already behind her. He covered her mouth with one hand and wrapped the other tightly around her waist.

"Don't say a word, and keep completely still," he hissed.

Gabby was puzzled. *Did he hear something? Is someone coming?*

Not that it mattered, since they were completely covered by the thick moss that hung down around them in a tight-knit group of cypress trees. Someone would have to practically be on top of them to know they were there at all.

And then, Gabby heard it—a buzzing noise, off in the distance. It grew louder as it came closer. It sounded like an industrial fan. Nash squeezed tighter around her mouth and waist. She had set the paddle down and didn't have much leverage. Even if someone was coming, there wasn't much she could do. They both stared out beyond the moss toward the noise.

Finally, she saw the outline of a boat making its way toward them. It was an airboat, and as it grew closer, Gabby could see at least three people on it. Nash pressed up against Gabby.

"If you try to scream or move and they see you, I will kill them all," Nash threatened, his voice infused with a coldness and an authority Gabby had never heard from him. "Nod your head if you understand."

Gabby slowly nodded and continued to stare forward. The boat was just fifty yards away, and she could see a captain perched up high with two others sitting on a bench in front of him.

Probably just an airboat tour, she thought. *But who does that on Christmas Eve? I wish they would see us.*

As the boat neared to twenty yards, Gabby got a clearer look at the people on the boat. It couldn't be . . . Nash squeezed harder, and before she knew it, they had passed her. But beneath the disappointment, hope fluttered within her. It was the first time since the wedding that she had laid eyes on Soojin and Cooper Smith.

***

The morning fog lifted as the airboat zipped across the thick, green water of the bayou. Cooper had his arm wrapped tightly around Soojin as they leaned into each other against the cold. They were both thankful for the lap belts as Leroy whipped around the big cypress trees. A few times, he cut the corners so close that they ended up covered with the moss that hung down from the trees.

After what seemed like an eternity, Leroy started to slow down. Cooper thought he had glimpsed a few alligators during the ride, but he couldn't be sure. He noticed Soojin was keeping her legs as far away from the edge of the boat as possible, just like he was.

There is no way I'm going back home with a peg leg, thought Cooper.

Leroy slowed the boat to a crawl. Both the moss and the cypress trees grew thick here, blocking out the sun. *Like something straight out of a movie.* Cooper's heart started to beat a little faster. *Can't wait to go home to some friendly bodies of water in Minnesota.*

Cooper realized now that finding the houseboat would only be half the battle.

What if Nash and Doyle are in there with Gabby? Are we really prepared to fight them to get her back? Cooper looked over at Soojin. *Well, maybe she is.*

Leroy cut the engine, and the airboat floated across the water. Cooper looked back at him, and he pointed to a patch of cypress trees on his left. Cooper tapped Soojin on the knee, showing her where Leroy was pointing.

It was nearly impossible to make out, but as they got closer Cooper saw the vague outline of what looked like a houseboat. It really was a perfect hideout—literally in the middle of the bayou, tucked into a patch of cypress trees that had so much moss hanging down you couldn't see past it.

Cooper took off his ear mufflers and seat belt and motioned for Soojin to do the same. He looked back up at Leroy and put his index finger over his mouth, signaling for him to be quiet.

Soojin leaned close and whispered, "Do you think it's the right houseboat?"

"Has to be," Cooper responded. "You ready?"

Soojin nodded, looking back toward the trees.

Leroy drifted the boat in around the trees until they finally got a good look at the houseboat wedged into the trees in the shadows. Cooper felt a tap on his shoulder and looked back to see Leroy pointing to a long metal paddle tied to the side of the airboat. Cooper unfastened it, using it to guide them to the houseboat.

The houseboat sat still and quiet. When they were within five feet of it, Soojin sprang from the airboat onto the houseboat's deck. Cooper scrambled to his feet and followed as the airboat slid right into the houseboat with a slight clash of metal-on-metal.

Soojin was already around the side of the houseboat, and she kicked in the door. Cooper rushed in behind her, his adrenaline high. He was ready to attack at the first sign of any hostile movement.

Cooper followed Soojin into the back room, searching the closet as Soojin looked under the bed. "Gabby!" she called. "Gabby! Are you here?"

They stopped to listen. Soojin returned to the main living area and found the ladder that led up to the ceiling. She climbed up and poked her head out. Cooper opened the bathroom and looked in the shower. Empty. Then he saw the note by the sink.

"Soojin! I've got something."

Soojin clattered down the ladder, stopping in the doorway to the bathroom when she saw Cooper reading the note. He handed it to Soojin.

It's Gabby. I'm alive. We left the houseboat on Xmas Eve by canoe. Not sure where we are going next, maybe Mexico. It's just Nash, he killed Doyle in ND.

"Oh my God." Soojin had to catch her breath. "It's her handwriting."

"She's alive," said Cooper. "Which means we just missed her if they left today. We could have passed them earlier."

Soojin tucked the letter in her pocket. "We have to go, now."

They sprinted out of the houseboat and jumped back onto the airboat. Leroy had a bewildered look on his face. "Start it up, Leroy, and take us back to our vehicle. Another two-hundred dollars in your pocket if you can spot a canoe with our friend in it along the way."

Leroy smiled. "Giddy up."

***

Gabby was still trying to process the fact that Soojin and Cooper were so close. Maybe they had discovered the letter and would come back. Gabby could barely hold the paddle now that they had started moving again; her hands were starting to blister. It seemed like they had paddled forever, and the morning sun was now high in the sky. They reached a canal that had a sign pointing toward the town of Dulac.

Gabby set her paddle across the front of the canoe, but Nash pushed on. Up ahead, Gabby saw a small marina connected to the canal. As they neared it, Gabby noticed several boats tied up to a series of docks. A small building faced the docks, but there were no vehicles parked there.

"Let me tell you what's about to happen." Nash's voice was direct and cold. "When we get to this dock, I'm going to go to the office and retrieve the key for one of the boats. In the meantime, I'm going to handcuff you to the dock. If you scream, I will duct tape your mouth until we arrive in Mexico. Do you understand?"

Gabby nodded.

"Good."

Nash maneuvered the canoe so it was parallel to the dock. He grabbed a rope and tied it to a post, securing the canoe. Gabby heard jingling behind her, and she turned around. Nash was moving toward her, the handcuffs dangling from one hand.

"Put your left arm out," he said.

"You don't have to handcuff me. I'm not going anywhere."

Nash rolled his eyes. "Remember what happened the last time I cut you some slack?"

Gabby reluctantly raised her arm. He handcuffed it to the rope on the dock. "I'll be right back."

Nash jumped up on the dock, heading straight toward the building. He peered into a window, then knocked on the door. He waited, but no one came. Then Nash positioned himself in front of the door. With one strong kick, the office door flew open. Gabby watched him rummage around inside, emerging with a handful of keys. He returned to inspect the various boats docked at the marina.

Gabby looked over her shoulder, praying for a sign of the airboat. But there wasn't another soul in sight.

Christmas Eve. Everyone is at home with their loved ones, and I'm stuck in Louisiana with this guy.

Nash was pulling the tarp off a fishing boat with two powerful engines. He tossed the tarp onto the dock and jumped into the boat. He fumbled with a few of the keys he'd grabbed from the office until the engines rumbled to life. Moving from one end of the boat to the other, he removed the ropes connecting it to the docks. Then he lowered the engines into the water and kicked off the dock. The boat slid into the water. He motored it toward Gabby.

"Hold onto this with your free hand." Nash tossed her a rope.

Gabby caught it and held tight. Nash eased down into the canoe and threw his bag into the boat. Then he unlocked Gabby's handcuff. She crawled up and over until she was sitting in the front of the boat. Nash climbed up behind her, jumping into the captain's seat. He backed the boat out so it was clear of the docks.

"Where are we going?" asked Gabby.

"There's a car stashed away at the marina in Houma. We'll take that to the sunshine state. From Florida, it's one boat ride across the gulf to our new life in Mexico. So, sit back and enjoy the ride." Nash smiled.

Gabby walked back from the front of the boat and sat down on the seat next to Nash. She hung her head, crossing her arms tightly across her body.

Please hurry, Soojin and Cooper. You're my last hope.

***

With every passing minute, Cooper and Soojin grew more anxious. Their eyes were strained from scanning the horizon and every shore and shadow for signs of the canoe or Gabby. Glancing at his phone, Cooper saw it was already 3 pm. It had taken most of the day to go out to the houseboat and get back to Leroy's marina—and the later it got, the harder it would be to catch up with Gabby.

Cooper looked over at Soojin and saw she was steely-eyed. Over his shoulder, Leroy continued to push the airboat's engines on full throttle. Leroy looked down at Cooper and pointed off into the distance. Cooper nodded.

At the edge of the canal, Cooper could vaguely make out Leroy's Landing. As they neared, they could see the boats tied to the docks and the office building where their minivan was parked. Soojin tugged at Cooper's leg and pointed at a boat tied to the dock. Cooper saw it right away. It wasn't the canoe they were looking for, but it was the only uncovered boat, and it hadn't been there that morning. Leroy had also followed Cooper and Soojin's gaze, but he just shrugged.

Leroy pulled the airboat in fast and turned down the throttle at the last moment so it would safely float in next to the new boat. It was a Lund fishing boat with two powerful engines. Soojin and Cooper unlatched their seatbelts and ripped off their ear mufflers as the airboat bumped up against the dock's buffers. Cooper threw the airboat's rope up on the dock's pole and jumped up.

Just then, a blue sedan came ripping out of the woods from the property adjacent to Leroy's Landing. Two occupants sat in the vehicle's front seat, and as it whizzed by them, Cooper caught a glimpse of Gabby.

Soojin jumped out of the boat and sprinted past Cooper. "That's them! We can't let them get away."

Cooper dashed after her toward the minivan. He pulled the keys out of his pocket, unlocking the van with the remote. As he opened the door, he looked back and saw Leroy smiling and waving.

"We'll be back to pay you!" Cooper shouted, jumping into the minivan.

Soojin was already in her seat and pulling her phone out of her pocket. "Hurry, hurry! We have to go!"

Cooper put the van in drive and took off after the sedan. By the time they reached the main road, Nash was already a few hundred meters ahead to their left. Cooper gunned it.

The one time I need a fast rental car, and we're in a minivan. Cooper shook his head. *Should have paid extra for the Mustang.*

"Faster, we have to catch them." Soojin dialed a number on her phone.

"Who are you calling?"

"911."

Cooper caught sight of a street sign. "Good, we are heading north on Grand Caillou Road."

"Got it."

Despite the slow acceleration speed, the van was cruising along now and gaining on the sedan. Cooper was going over 100 mph, and the van was handling it well. Soojin put her phone on speaker as it dialed 911.

A female operator answered after two rings. "911 emergency services. How can I help you?"

"We are in pursuit of a kidnapper who has our friend," said Soojin.

"What is your location?" asked the operator.

"We are south of Houma heading north on Grand Caillou Road."

"Do you have a cross street?"

Soojin looked over at Cooper and back out at the sedan. "They're turning," said Cooper. "Hold on one moment."

"We are getting into Houma now," said Soojin. "We are about to turn, I'll let you know what street."

"What is your name?" asked the operator.

"My name is Soojin Smith, and I'm with Cooper Smith."

"Please describe the situation."

"We are trying to get our friend Gabby Hanson back; she was kidnapped a few weeks ago in North Dakota by a man named Declan Nash. We are in vehicle pursuit of them right now. They are driving a blue Ford Taurus sedan."

Cooper made a sharp turn.

"We're on Prospect Boulevard," said Soojin. "Just turned off of Grand Caillou Road onto Prospect."

"Ma'am, we have your position and will dispatch a unit. Please slow down and stop your vehicle and allow the authorities to take over."

Soojin looked over at Cooper, who was shaking his head. "There is no way I'm stopping until I see a police officer take Nash down," said Cooper.

"I'm sorry, we can't do that," said Soojin.

"Ma'am, this is serious. You could be hurt or killed. Please stand down and let the authorities take over."

"It's Christmas Eve!" shouted Soojin. "You probably have three police officers working in the whole state of Louisiana! We will not stop until Nash is caught."

Cooper was now about one-hundred yards behind Nash. They were approaching a T-intersection, and Nash slowed down and turned right. Cooper followed him, glancing at the sign. "We just turned right on 182."

"How far out are your officers?" asked Soojin.

"Mrs. Smith, I assure you they are on their way. I called all available units in that area to respond."

Cooper was holding steady at around one hundred yards behind Nash as they both maneuvered around a UPS delivery truck. Traffic was light because of the holiday. "Looks like he may be getting onto the highway up ahead," said Cooper.

"The kidnapper is merging onto Highway 90 East," said Soojin. "Toward New Orleans."

There was no response from the operator.

"Did you hear me?" asked Soojin.

"Yes, I heard you," said the operator. "I just talked to an officer who is located just east of your position on US 90 East. This officer will be able to take it from here. Please stop your vehicle."

"Screw it." Soojin turned off her phone. "We found her, we can get her back, too."

Cooper nodded, his foot pressed so hard on the accelerator that it touched the floor. His knuckles were white, his eyes laser-focused on the blue sedan in front of them.

"Up there, on the right," said Cooper.

"I see it," said Soojin.

A police car sat on the side of the road a quarter of a mile ahead of them, lights flashing. Nash pulled around a semi-truck and stayed in the left lane. Cooper came up behind them and watched the police car pull out into the right lane. The police car sped up but Nash was going too fast and passed it.

Cooper slowed down for a moment to let the police car pull in front of him. Then he sped back up and looked down at the speedometer, which read 110 mph.

"You have your seatbelt on, right?" asked Cooper.

"Yes, don't worry about me. Just stay with them."

Nash pulled his vehicle into the right lane while the police car moved into the left lane, even with Nash.

"Come on, get him," said Cooper.

"What's he going to do?" asked Soojin.

Before the police officer could make a move, Nash turned his wheels sharply to the left and smashed into the police car. The force of the collision caused the police car to fishtail, and then it was heading sideways into the median.

"No, no, no!" shouted Soojin.

The police car caught a patch of grass and shot up in the sky as it started to barrel-roll uncontrollably.

"Soojin, call an ambulance."

Nash pulled back over in front of Cooper and blocked his path as he kept his speed up.

Soojin put her phone back on speakerphone and the same female operator answered. "911 emergency services. How can I help you?"

"It's Soojin Smith again. Your officer's vehicle just went off the road on 90 East and barrel-rolled into the median."

"What is your location?"

"We are coming up on a bridge that is going over a river or canal," said Soojin. "There are no signs, though."

They raced over the bridge as Cooper stayed with Nash.

"We just went over the bridge, and there is a sign that says St. Charles Parish," said Soojin.

"Let me see if I can find you," said the operator.

"Here's another sign," said Cooper.

"We are at the junction with Louisiana road number 632."

"Okay, great," said the operator. "For the last time, please pull over and let our officers do the rest."

"Gotta go." Soojin turned off her phone again. "Gabby is right in front of us, and there is no way I'm stopping now. I don't care if the president was on the line."

Cooper's adrenaline was sky high, but his knuckles were starting to hurt from gripping the steering wheel so hard.

"Where do you think he's headed?" asked Cooper.

"Woah!"

A truck suddenly pulled off of a side road onto the highway and Cooper had to jerk the wheel to avoid a collision. The minivan fishtailed for a few moments before it regained its traction.

At any moment they could lose Nash—and with him, Gabby. Thankfully, Cooper saw the lights of another police car in the distance. Nash must have seen it, too, because he exited suddenly off of 90 for Interstate 310 North. Cooper turned at the last second and followed him.

"The police car saw us exit; he's coming across the median now," reported Soojin.

"Good, but it'll take him forever to catch up. We are doing well over a hundred still." Cooper's shoulders were tense as he strained to keep his hands tightly wrapped around the steering wheel.

In the rearview mirror, Cooper could see the police car making its way to the chase, but it was still too far back. After a few more minutes, they arrived at another bridge.

"No way," said Soojin.

"What?"

"We are about to cross the Mississippi River."

Cooper and Soojin lived close to the Mississippi in Saint Paul, and spent a lot of time on or near the river back home.

"Do you think he's going all the way into New Orleans?" asked Cooper.

"Sure looks that way," said Soojin. "We can't let him get away."

***

Gabby clutched the handle above her window with her right hand and her seatbelt with her left as Nash raced on. As they crossed over the Mississippi, a memory of her time rowing on the river for the Minnesota Gophers back in college flashed through her mind. Over her shoulder she could still see the minivan, although the sun was starting to set and it skewed her vision.

"Keep your eyes forward, and hold on," ordered Nash.

A truck suddenly moved into the left lane in front of them, and Nash had to maneuver around it on the shoulder, hugging the median and guardrail. Gabby's body jerked to the side. Once he was around the truck, he pulled out in front of it. The left lane spread out empty in front of them, and they passed the slower-moving cars in the right lane as if they were parked. Nash let out a deep breath.

"I saw how you looked at those people in the boat earlier," he said. "Now they're in the minivan behind us. Do you know them?"

Gabby crossed her arms and didn't respond.

"I know you do," Nash pressed. "I saw your reaction when you saw them. Who are they?"

This guy thinks he can boss me around, and now he wants me to open up?

"I'm sorry I've been so cold and direct today," he said. "I just need you to do exactly as I say so we can get out of here together in one piece."

"What exactly is your plan now?" Gabby asked.

"We will still go to Florida, but not in this car," Nash said. "The authorities will be looking for it now. I know a guy who lives in downtown New Orleans, and he owes me a huge favor on account of me looking the other way on some of his criminal activity when he lived in Texas and I was working for the Rangers. If we can get to his place, we can hide out until things blow over."

"How do you know if he is even there?" asked Gabby.

"Don't worry about that; I arranged this back-up plan before we even left North Dakota, so we will be just fine once we get there." Nash looked up at the rearview mirror and saw the minivan was still trailing them. "We just need to ditch this minivan and make sure there aren't any more cops that get in our way."

"Don't you feel bad about running that police officer off the road back there?"

"Look, it was either him or us. Like I said, this will all blow over soon. We just need to get to the safe house. Oh, shoot."

"What?"

"Another police car up ahead," said Nash. "Looks like two of them, actually."

The police cars stood on either side of the interstate with their lights on. One of the officers was pulling something out of his trunk.

"He's grabbing spikes, hold on." Nash pushed down the gas as hard as it would go, swerving toward the center lane. The police officer threw the spikes, but they landed short and Nash dodged around them.

Gabby turned around and looked out the back window. Cooper and Soojin swerved around the spike strip as well, keeping on their tail. The second police car was already accelerating after them from the shoulder, and the officer who threw the strip was running to his vehicle to join the pursuit.

Come on guys, stay on us.

"Hold on tight." Nash exited at the last second and barely missed a vehicle that tried to exit at the same time.

They were now on Interstate 10 East heading toward New Orleans. A green exit sign read *N.O. Intl Airport 1 ¾ MILES.* Nash darted across all three of the highway's lanes, narrowly missing other cars. His eyes were alight, his body quivering with energy.

He's enjoying this, Gabby realized.

The wail of sirens flooded Gabby's ears. Two police cars had now caught up with them. They pulled in front of the minivan so they were directly behind them and closing.

Nash looked up in the rearview mirror again. "Let's have some fun."

At the last possible second, he turned off the interstate, driving over the white warning track and barely missing a metal guardrail as he took Exit 223 for the airport. One of the police cars couldn't make the sharp turn and skidded out of control past them on the interstate. The other one slowed way down and made the exit, but at the expense of a growing distance between them. The Smiths trailed the procession in the minivan.

"We'll make them think we are headed to the airport. They'll really scramble now." Nash laughed.

Nash turned right onto Williams Boulevard with one police car and the minivan behind him. Once he cleared the intersection and guardrail, he jerked the car left so it was directly facing a narrow part of the median, about the height of a curb.

"Get ready."

Gabby held on tight. Nash lurched the car forward. At an angle, they bumped and scraped their way over the median, narrowly missing an oncoming car in the other lane. Nash then turned the car so they were heading the other direction on Williams Boulevard.

As they sped up, Gabby could clearly see both the police car and the Smiths in the minivan braking hard. They both turned and tried the same maneuver. Gabby couldn't tell, but she thought they both made it over the median, although it slowed them way down.

Nash accelerated the car quickly back on the on ramp for Interstate 10 East. He checked the mirror before pushing the gas to the floor and training his eyes on the horizon as the sun set behind them.

When he slows down, I'll make a break for it, thought Gabby, *because there is no way in hell I'm going to be locked up in a safe house with him.* Gabby looked over at Nash out of the corner of her eye.

"The Big Easy." Nash smiled. "Here we come."

***

The minivan was firing on all cylinders, but it took the rest of the interstate from the airport to the city of New Orleans to be within eyesight of the blue Ford Taurus. The second police car they had lost at the airport earlier had now caught up and Cooper drove at a close but safe distance behind them as they pursued Nash. Cooper wondered for a minute if he might get picked up for speeding or reckless driving, but realized the police were more focused on the kidnapper's vehicle.

"Where do you think he's going to go?" asked Soojin.

"No idea," said Cooper. "And this is our first time to New Orleans, so we are at a huge disadvantage."

"Do you think they'll leave the car at some point?"

"It's possible, so we have to be ready, too," said Cooper.

"It just got a whole lot more difficult with the sun going down. See if you can get any closer."

"I would," said Cooper. "But I don't think those police officers want us any closer than we are now. Actually, I'm pretty sure they wouldn't want us driving like this at all."

"We'll worry about that later," said Soojin. "Just inch closer if you can."

Cooper tried to speed up, but there was a natural turn in the road as Interstate 10 curved to the left. "Look at that. I think he's exiting."

"You're right, get over in the right lane."

Traffic started to pick up as they neared New Orleans. The police sirens and lights caused the other cars to move over so Cooper didn't have to fight with traffic on the single-lane exit—until a car pulled back out unexpectedly from the shoulder behind the police and in front of Cooper. Cooper veered left to avoid the car, smashing the minivan against the left guardrail. The van bounced off the rail and hit the merging car.

Cooper held the steering wheel tight and powered the van through the collision as they regained their composure.

"You okay?" Cooper asked. He sped back up to stay with the other fleeing vehicles.

Soojin rubbed her neck. "Yeah, I'm fine. Just a little whiplash."

They were now off of the interstate racing down Basin Street.

"There's another curve up ahead to the right," said Soojin.

"I see it," said Cooper. "Hold on."

They edged around some cars with the minivan as the road veered to the right.

"Oh, no. Get over now!" Soojin pointed across the median. "He did another U-turn, we have to get over there."

Cooper sharply turned the wheel to the left, following a path that opened up from the police car in front of him. He could see Nash heading the other direction across the median, then suddenly Nash turned again.

"Hurry. He just went right," said Soojin.

"Got it," said Cooper.

"Turn right here," said Soojin. "Onto Toulousse Street."

It was a small, one-way street, and Cooper saw red lights at an intersection up ahead. Nash sped through, barely escaping a collision with a pickup truck. The first police car was not so lucky. The truck T-boned it, slamming it away from the intersection. The second police car swerved to the right and ended up crashing into the light pole.

Cooper slowed down, narrowly missing rear-ending the second police car as he swerved to the left and then back to the right to stay on Toulousse. The road narrowed even further here, and Cooper tried to avoid rear-ending parked cars as he stayed on Nash.

A string of cars was stopped at an intersection up ahead. Nash swerved over on the sidewalk to pass them. Pedestrians screamed and jumped out of the way. Cooper followed Nash's path, slowing down to avoid hitting a sign on the sidewalk, and honking his horn to alert pedestrians.

Nash proceeded to worm his way down Toulouse Street, barely missing cars, pedestrians, and signs in the heavily trafficked tourist part of downtown New Orleans. The famous two- and three-story old brick buildings of the French Quarter hugged the sidewalk. Christmas lights hung from the second-floor balconies, where people leaned over railings watching the commotion below.

Cooper clutched the wheel and maneuvered around another car until he was directly behind Nash. "Get ready. If they make a break for it on foot, we'll lose them down here in this maze."

"There's a stoplight up there," said Soojin. "Which way is he turning?"

Nash reached the stoplight and pointed the Ford's nose to the right, then quickly jerked the car to the left. Cooper accelerated behind him as they turned left onto Decatur Street. Despite it being Christmas Eve, clusters of people still walked along the street.

The buildings cleared up ahead, and Cooper saw trees illuminated with Christmas lights. "What's this area?"

"Coming up on Jackson Square," said Soojin. "Look, police cars."

Two police cars flanked Decatur Street, their lights flashing. Nash hit his brakes and pulled his car to the left, stopping right in front of a string of horse-drawn carriages at the entrance of the square. The horses spooked, darting out in different directions with or without their masters in tow. People had paused to gawk as the driver's side door opened and Nash stumbled out.

"Here we go," said Cooper. Soojin's hand was already on her door latch.

Cooper caught a glimpse of Gabby as she tried to sprint out of her door, but Nash grabbed her wrist, pointing a gun in her face as he yanked her toward him. Then he shot once into the air and fired another round right at the minivan. It hit the window between Cooper and Soojin, and they both ducked as Cooper stopped the van.

"Go, go, go!" shouted Cooper.

They jumped out of the van into chaos. People screamed and ran in every direction. The horses shrieked, clattering through the square with empty carts behind them. The police drove straight toward the van.

Nash dragged Gabby into Jackson Square as Soojin sprinted behind them. Cooper followed alongside to the left. Nash stopped briefly at a giant statute of a man riding a horse in the center of the square. With an arm locked around Gabby's neck, he fired once toward Soojin. She dove out of the way behind a tree.

Cooper froze when he heard the gunshot and his eyes darted toward Soojin to see if she was okay. When he saw her safe behind a tree, he started running again until he was even with the statue. Nash took off again with Gabby around the other side of the statue, and now they were headed toward the big white cathedral at the end of the square.

Dozens of confused Christmas carolers stood between the cathedral and a fountain at the far end of the square. They were holding candles, glancing around in search of the source of the excitement. Halfway to the fountain, Nash shot another round up into the air. The carolers scattered, tripping over each other and blocking the square's exit. Nash scrambled back from the fountain, dragging Gabby with him.

It was all the time Cooper needed. He closed on Nash and Gabby, tackling them both to the ground in front of the fountain. Cooper reached for Nash's gun, but Nash squeezed off a round that hit Cooper in the front of his left shoulder. The bullet knocked Cooper back, but he clutched Gabby's wrist with his right arm and pulled her with him.

Nash slid back and aimed at Cooper again, but Gabby twisted her body to shield him, taking the bullet in her right forearm. Nash froze, his face horror-stricken, then tried to yank Gabby back.

Cooper watched as Soojin came up behind Nash, sending a flying sidekick into the small of his back. He dropped to his knees, then pivoted toward her with the gun.

A fast counter punch by Soojin knocked the gun away, and she attempted to follow it with a straight kick to Nash's face. He ducked, then spun with a leg sweep that knocked Soojin to the ground.

Cooper clutched his shoulder as he pulled Gabby around the side of the fountain. Police officers ran toward them from across the square. He squirmed back around to see if he could help Soojin.

Soojin leapt up from the ground and dodged a punch from Nash. They spun back around at each other. Nash jabbed at Soojin with his left arm and sent a would-be knockout right hook to her head. But she ducked just in time and elbowed him in the ribs as his momentum took him past her. She then kicked the back of the leg he had planted on, and he collapsed to his knees.

Cooper found Nash's gun lying on the ground by the fountain, and he dove for it. Clutching his injured shoulder, he scooped up the handgun with his good arm.

Soojin attempted a finishing blow to the back of Nash's head, but he ducked as her kick sailed over him. He used her momentum to throw her to the ground. Nash then turned and, with a limp, tried to run past Cooper and the approaching policemen.

Nash was all but ten feet away when Cooper lined up the sights with his one good arm and pulled the trigger. The bullet hit Nash behind his right knee and exploded out the front of his kneecap. He dropped on his face into the pavement.

"Drop the gun, drop the gun!" shouted out the police officers.

Cooper obeyed, returning his hand to his injured shoulder.

"That's him!" Soojin pointed. "The one on the ground is Nash; arrest him."

The officers ran past the fountain and handcuffed a slithering Nash as blood spilled out from his leg.

Soojin ran over to Cooper. "Are you okay?"

"Yes, let's go check on Gabby."

They found Gabby propped up against the side of the fountain, clutching her bleeding arm.

Soojin called over at the police officers, who were now kneeling on top of Nash. "Call an ambulance—we have two more wounded over here."

"They're on their way," replied one of the officers.

Soojin and Cooper sat on either side of Gabby, their eyes filling with tears as the three of them embraced.

CHAPTER 24

Saint Paul, Minnesota

Cooper stood on the sidewalk of Cedar Street in downtown Saint Paul, directly across from MPR headquarters. It had been just over a month since Gabby had reunited with her family—and, as promised, Senator Hanson had arrived in Saint Paul to do an exclusive interview with Cooper. Before he went inside, Cooper waited for the top of the scrolling headlines for his daily moment of Zen.

> *Monday, January 26, 2015 –*
> *Price of Oil Drops to $45 a*
> *Barrel for the First Time Since*
> *April 2009; Oil Industry in*
> *Disarray...*

Sweet justice, thought Cooper.

Cooper used to take his morning smoke here on the sidewalk as he watched the first headline, but he was glad to have kicked the habit again. He was down to one pack of Juicy Fruit gum a day. He blew a bubble in the cool morning air, popping it with his lips as he crossed the street and entered work through the main door.

His left arm was still in a sling, but the pain didn't bother him so much anymore, and he was looking forward to rehab. He started walking up to the third floor, then stopped on the second flight of stairs. Something caught his eye, and he turned to look out the large glass panel windows across the street.

It can't be. Is that the black Dodge Charger from before?

The Charger was idling across the street on Fort Road, with a man inside it on his telephone.

Wheeler.

Cooper waved, but Wheeler turned his head and pretended not to be watching.

You're too late. The interview is today, and now you're out of a job.

***

Governor Simmons' secretary immediately patched the call through to him.

"How bad is it?" asked Simmons.

"It's not looking good," said Wheeler. "Hanson already arrived at the studio, and the reporter just went inside. The interview is going to happen today."

Simmons slammed his fist down on the table. "I paid you to take care of this."

"Look, I don't do hit jobs, so what else do you want from me?"

"What am I suppose to do now?" demanded Simmons.

"Governor, I suggest you either find yourself an excellent lawyer or you get to Mexico as quickly as possible. Same for Thompson."

"You no good—"

There was a click on the other end of the line, and Simmons slammed his phone down on his desk. His Nixon bobblehead doll shook its head at him.

"Oh, shut up!" Simmons hurled Nixon across the room, where it smashed against his office door. A loud knock followed.

"Go away, it was nothing," said Simmons.

The door swung open. Two FBI agents entered, flashing their badges. The first one presented a search warrant to Simmons while the second started handcuffing him.

"What—what is the—the meaning of this?" Simmons stammered.

"Rick Simmons, you are under arrest for bribery, fraud, and corruption. You have the right to remain silent . . ."

Simmons zoned out the rest of his Miranda rights and let the officers drag him out of his office, his head hung low. When he reached his door, he saw Nixon laying on the ground in pieces.

***

Lisa Larson was slumped down in a chair in front of Bill Anderson's desk when Cooper entered Bill's office.

"It's about time you got here," said Bill. "We were getting ready to scratch your interview."

"And give up the story of the year? That would be a big mistake!" Cooper smiled at Larson. She rolled her eyes.

"Just sit down so we can go through the program," said Bill.

Cooper took the seat beside Larson.

"Okay, so we are going to put you on News Presents today at noon." Bill pointed at Lisa. "The first thirty minutes of the show will be Larson's special from her interviews and discoveries out in North Dakota." Bill then turned to Cooper. "The second thirty minutes of the show will be your live interview of Senator Hanson. *Comprendé*?"

"That's fine," said Lisa.

"Works for me," said Cooper.

"We will wait to see how the reception of the story is today," said Bill. "If it is positive, we will play more of your

North Dakota reporting and clips from your interview the rest of the week as a miniseries. Do you have your questions ready?"

Cooper nodded. "Yes, but I think we'll just have to turn the microphone on and let the senator do the talking."

Bill shook his head. "You young punks are always looking for the easy way out of everything. Back in my day—"

"I know what you're going to say," interjected Cooper. "You typed on an old typewriter and carried it to and from work uphill both ways in the snow!"

Bill pointed to the door. "Get out. Get out right now, Cooper Smith. I've made it twenty-six days without a blowup this year for my New Year's resolution, and I'm not about to waste one on you. Just deliver the story, or you can kiss the investigative team goodbye."

Lisa smiled as she got up and quickly left the office. Cooper followed and touched her on the shoulder.

She spun. "What?" She had one hand on her hip.

"Hey, I just wanted to say, whatever happens with that investigative slot . . . well, may the best reporter win." Cooper stuck his hand out.

Lisa sneered. "Save the handshake for your next job interview after you get the pink slip here." She turned to walk away, but then stopped.

Facing Cooper again, she said, "Okay, whatever, good luck." She shook his hand, then darted away before he could respond.

Cooper laughed.

Of all the reporters on this earth, the radio gods had to pair me up with someone from Wisconsin.

***

The producers decided to use the UBS Forum studio for Senator Hanson's interview. The Forum was one of MPR's newest studios, and it was designed to look and feel like a small theatre, with elevated seating for the audience. A huge glass window behind the stage looked out on the Central Presbyterian Church in the foreground, and the state capitol building in the background.

Two sofa chairs faced each other on the stage, angled slightly toward the audience. Mark walked onto the stage and shook Cooper's hand, and then the two of them took their seats. The countdown in the studio began as Lisa's segment was ending. Cooper looked out and saw Soojin sitting next to Gabby in the audience. They were both glowing. Like Cooper, Gabby wore her arm in a sling. She pointed to it and winked at him. Cooper gave her a thumbs-up and smiled at Soojin as the studio lights came on and the house lights dimmed.

Cooper looked up to the control room and was surprised to see Bill Anderson standing next to Lisa. Bill pointed two fingers to his eyes and then pointed his index finger right back at Cooper. Cooper nodded; the message was clear. Lisa frowned, her arms crossed over her chest.

If this interview goes well, I just might be able to get that investigative team position, thought Cooper. But before he could do any more dreaming, the red light indicating they were live turned on.

"Welcome to this special edition of Minnesota Public Radio News Presents, coming live from the UBS Forum studio in downtown Saint Paul. My name is Cooper Smith, and I have the privilege to be sitting here today with Senator Mark Hanson, one of North Dakota's longest-serving state senators from District One in Williston." Cooper looked up at Mark. "It's a pleasure having you in the studio today."

"It's certainly a pleasure to be here," said Mark. "Thanks for having me on your show."

"We have a lot to discuss, so let's dive right in. Now, for our listeners who haven't heard, last month the Senator's granddaughter, Gabby Hanson, was kidnapped from the

Williston recreation center. After several weeks in captivity, she was able to escape and is with us here today."

The studio audience started clapping, and Cooper looked out at them and smiled. The stage manager had instructed them to be quiet before the show began, but Cooper didn't mind the applause. When the noise died down, he looked back at Mark.

"Can you talk about what was going through your mind while Gabby was gone, and discuss a little bit about what you want to share with our listeners today?"

"Well, we all have you and Soojin to thank for getting Gabby back. Words can't express our family's gratitude for your help. Now, in order to understand how my wife Sydney and I handled Gabby's disappearance, it is important to start way back at the beginning. Do you mind if I give a little background?"

"Not at all."

"Thanks." Mark shifted in his chair and looked out at the audience. "I was born in Williston, and I've lived there my whole life. I grew up on the farm, and I remember when I was a small child we used to have these slick oilmen come to our home and talk to us about buying the rights to our land. They said there was going to be a huge oil boom, and we would all get rich if we sold right now. My father never would sell, but plenty of our neighbors did. Some of them made some money, but most of them lost out big. When the first bust happened shortly after in the fifties, many of those farmers tried to buy back the land but were forced to pay four or five times the original price. They went bankrupt. Our happy community was literally ripped apart as we watched families we grew up with suddenly leave. You know what I kept from that time?"

Mark was such a good storyteller Cooper almost forgot he was interviewing him live on the air. "What'd you keep?"

"I kept a *Life* magazine from the year 1951. In that magazine is a picture of a farmer sitting on his tractor with a look of consternation as an oilman extends a pen for him to sign his land away. I still have that picture as a reminder all these years later. And, sure enough, thirty years later in the early 1980s, a second wave of oil mania hit western North Dakota. At that point, I was farming the same land my father used to farm. And, just like before, slick oilmen would come and try to offer me the world to buy my land, or at least the mineral rights to it. I didn't budge, but once again a lot of our neighbors did. When the industry went belly-up a few years later, the oil workers all left and the remaining folks in the community had to pick up the pieces."

"Is that what inspired you to go into politics?" asked Cooper.

Mark nodded. "You got it. I couldn't sit around anymore and watch our community fall apart. I mean, we invested in public works and accommodations for the out-of-state oil companies and workers just to watch them vanish the second the oil dried up. I was elected in 1984 to the state senate, and I have been serving there ever since trying to make a better future for our grandchildren, and hopefully for their grandchildren after them."

"So, you must have felt torn when a new oil technique, known as fracking, led to the third and current Bakken boom, which started back in the mid 2000s."

"You're right," said Mark. "I couldn't believe how fast and furious this third boom came on. It dwarfed the other two in its size and impact on the state.

"And then came the vote in 2009 to give major tax breaks to oil companies entering the North Dakota market."

Mark looked down and shook his head. "Having the honor to serve in our state's senate for three decades, I've literally pushed the green button for yes, or the red one for no, thousands of times. You can't imagine how badly I wanted to push the red button on that vote, but I knew it would cost me if I did, so I pushed green. One of my colleagues, a prominent, long-standing senator, pushed the red button. He was crucified in radio and television advertisements during his 2010 reelection campaign. They labeled him as being a man that hated the Bakken, they even called him a tree hugger! Can you imagine this? I assure you he was nothing of the sort. He lost that election and the next one in 2012."

Cooper leaned forward in his chair. "Okay, so you voted for the tax break and you kept your seat. What has happened since?"

Mark paused. "Well, it used to be that if you grew up in rural North Dakota, there was a good chance you would be working out on the farm. Maybe taking it over one day from your parents. Now, some of the local kids are joining the oil industry. Sure, some of them get in and earn a quick buck, and then use it to buy cows or pay cash for more modern equipment to make life a little easier on the farm. Others decide to make a career of it, and they work their way up the ladder from being the worm to the driller to who knows what. But, one of the biggest changes has been the influx of workers from other states and even other countries. These workers may stay for months and even years on end, but the vast majority of them are transient workers. They leave their families and live out of trucks and man camps. They do spend some money locally, but most of it goes back home to wherever they came from. Along with these workers have come the issues of increased crime, drugs, violence, rising housing costs, infrastructure problems, and lack of medical care. The list goes on."

Cooper looked down and read from his notes. "The price of oil dropped to forty-five dollars a barrel today. New reports coming out of Williston are saying some of the man camps in western North Dakota are already clearing out and that oil companies are starting to leave." Cooper looked back up at Mark. "Is this third boom sustainable?"

Mark shook his head. "It'll be a different bust from the last ones, but I assure you it's about to get pretty rough for certain leaders and oil companies in North Dakota."

Cooper gave Mark a puzzled look. "What do you mean by that?"

Mark took a deep breath and exhaled. "In 1998, my son and daughter-in-law were killed by a drunk driver who swerved into their lane and hit them head-on. They were Gabby's parents, and the senseless loss of life affected all of us greatly. Soon after, Sydney and I started a nonprofit organization that fought to keep drunk drivers off the roads in North Dakota. It was like a local version of Mothers Against Drunk Driving, if you've heard of that foundation."

"I have."

"As with any nonprofit, we worked hard to get donations. We used the money for public service announcements aimed at promoting designated driver programs, and for giving people ways to anonymously report on drunk-drivers—since many times it was friends or family members involved. Shortly after the oil company tax break vote in 2009, I noticed our nonprofit started receiving a large uptick in donations. Most of the donations were anonymous, but a few came from some senior members of the political leadership in North Dakota. Namely, Rick Simmons and Nate Thompson, who are the current governor and lieutenant governor of North Dakota. We happily took their money and all the other donations and put it to good use." Mark looked up to the ceiling in disgust. "I should have known there were strings attached."

"What kind of strings?" Cooper looked up at the control room and saw Bill keenly looking down. Lisa had her hands on her hips, but her face showed that her interest had also been roused.

"The two of them were elected to their current positions in 2010," said Mark. "In the summer of 2011, they asked me to join them for a private meeting in the governor's office. At that meeting, they told me all of the money pouring into our nonprofit was oil-bribe money. The oil companies were paying them to look the other way on certain projects, or to bend rules to help select companies out. They wanted to use my influence in Williston, the epicenter of the Bakken, as a way to pad their pockets and help their oil companies out."

Cooper sat up in surprise. "What'd you do?"

Mark hung his head. "I looked the other way. They had blackmailed me right into it, and I was stuck. They swore they would leak to the press how our nonprofit was taking oil-bribe money." When Mark looked back up at Cooper, he had rage in his eyes. "They corrupted me, and got rich doing it."

Cooper couldn't believe the senator was admitting this on live radio. "What sorts of things would they do for the oil companies?"

"They would redraw protected state and federal land lines so areas would be unaccounted for. The oil companies would suddenly swoop in and open up a new drill right next to a supposedly protected river, or public land. They even managed to pull the rug out from under the Department of the Interior and were able to get oil drills set up right on the border of the Teddy Roosevelt National Park. And with fracking, they didn't just drill straight down. No, those companies drilled down and then sideways, right under one of our National Parks."

Cooper suppressed a gasp. He looked up at a smiling Bill and a frowning Lisa in the control room before turning back to Mark. "And you're saying that Governor Simmons and Lieutenant Governor Thompson facilitated all of this?"

Mark nodded. "Yes."

"Senator," said Cooper, "if what you're saying is true, then you could also be implicated and arrested right along with Simmons and Thompson."

"That's right," agreed Mark. "But you see, something happened." He looked out at the audience. "My precious

Gabby was taken from us. Kidnapped, by out-of-state oil workers. Something finally snapped in me, and I knew what I had to do."

"Which was?"

"Most of the oil companies who were paying the bribes were from out of state, and even from other countries. I knew that no law enforcement agency in North Dakota would touch this, so I reached out to the FBI, and they put me in touch with an agent who specializes in white-collar crimes. I helped them build a case, and with my full cooperation, the FBI and U.S. Attorney's office have assured me that no charges will be pressed against me or anyone tied to our nonprofit organization. And the reason I am able to tell you this is they just informed me this morning that Governor Simmons, Lieutenant Thompson, and the corrupt employees of the oil companies have all been arrested."

Up in the control room, Bill Anderson flashed Cooper two thumbs-up while Lisa turned to leave.

"You're telling us the governor and lieutenant governor of North Dakota have just been arrested?" Cooper repeated.

"Yes, and rightfully so," said Mark. "North Dakota deserves better, and we must hold our leaders accountable. I said it to Thompson, and I'll tell it to you all now. The oil, to me, is just black gold. Let me repeat, it's *dirty black* gold. These people sold their souls to the devil for money and power. They used their positions to get rich off of oil bribes, and then used the money to help them get reelected. Am I perfect? No. I could have and should have done more to stop it. For that, I take full responsibility. I've made amends to my wife and to the Lord. As for Simmons, Thompson, and the others, well, I'm reminded of an old proverb my father used to tell me when I was a kid. He used to say, 'Son, what does it profit a man to gain the whole world but to lose his soul?'" Mark paused. "That always stuck with me, and I think it sums up this situation pretty well."

"What will you do now?"

Mark looked like a huge burden had just been lifted off his back. "I'm resigning as the senator of North Dakota's First District, and I plan to do everything in my power to help get my beautiful granddaughter elected to my seat." Mark smiled at Gabby.

Cooper checked the control room. Bill was waving his hand in a "wrap-it-up-while-you're-still-ahead" signal. Only sixty seconds remained of the time allotted for the interview.

Did I just punch my ticket to the investigative team? God, I hope so.

Cooper turned his attention back to Mark. "That was quite the story, Senator Hanson, and we want to thank you for coming all the way down here for this special interview." They shook hands, and then Cooper looked out on the audience. "And, thanks to our listeners for joining in on this special edition of MPR News Presents. Make sure to tell all your friends that you heard about it first on MPR, the rough-and-tumble story of *Black Gold in North Dakota*."

ACKNOWLEDGEMENTS

This book would not have been possible without the support and encouragement from my beloved family and cherished friends in all my creative endeavors. Also, words cannot express my gratitude to editor Lacey Louwagie for her professional advice and assistance in polishing this manuscript. Although the final editorial decisions are all my own, Lacey provided valuable guidance. A special thanks to the kindred spirits of Minnesota for making our home the greatest state in all the land. Lastly, the most important acknowledgement goes to the Lord for His many blessings.

ABOUT THE WRITER

Field's debut book, *Brown Sugar in Minnesota*, is a crime thriller that introduces Minnesota Public Radio reporter Cooper Smith as he faces a drug network in the North Star State. Smith then encounters the rough and tumble oil country in Field's sequel, *Black Gold in North Dakota*.

Field has also written over 50 songs and features 10 of them on his album *Great Lakes Legends*, a collection of songs inspired by American tall tales.

A Minnesota native, Field enjoys traveling the world and exploring America's national parks. Field is also a cold-brew coffee craftsman, brewing and bottling his signature Paul Bunyan Coffee blend.

joefield.net
amazon.com/author/joefield
twitter.com/JoeFieldWriter
goodreads.com/JoeFieldWriter

ALSO BY WRITER

COOPER SMITH BOOKS

Brown Sugar in Minnesota (1)
Black Gold in North Dakota (2)

MUSIC ALBUMS

Great Lakes Legends

Made in the USA
Lexington, KY
29 July 2017